The Infinite
Arena

SEVEN SCIENCE FICTION STORIES
ABOUT SPORTS

The Infinite
Arena

edited by Terry Carr

THOMAS NELSON INC., PUBLISHERS
Nashville
New York

All rights reserved under International and Pan-American Conventions. Published in Nashville, Tennessee, by Thomas Nelson, Inc., Publishers, and simultaneously in Don Mills, Ontario, by Thomas Nelson & Sons (Canada) Limited. Manufactured in the United States of America.

First edition

Library of Congress Cataloging in Publication Data

Main entry under title:

The Infinite arena.

   CONTENTS: Anderson, P. and Dickson, G. R. Joy in Mudville.—Jameson, M. Bullard reflects.—Laumer, K. The body builders. [etc.]
   1. Science fiction, American. 2. Sports—Fiction. I. Carr, Terry.
PZ1.I49 [PS648.S3]   813'.0876   76-30758
ISBN 0-8407-6538-X

Acknowledgments

JOY IN MUDVILLE by Poul Anderson and Gordon R. Dickson. Copyright 1955 by Fantasy House, Inc. From *Fantasy and Science Fiction*, by permission of the authors and their agents, Scott Meredith Literary Agency, Inc., 845 Third Ave., New York, N.Y. 10022.

BULLARD REFLECTS by Malcolm Jameson. Copyright 1941 by Street & Smith Publications, Inc.; copyright renewed © 1969 by Condé Nast Publications Inc. From *Astounding Science-Fiction*, by arrangement with Forrest J Ackerman, 2495 Glendower Ave., Hollywood CA 90027, for the Estate of Malcolm Jameson.

Contents

Introduction

Our sports are constantly changing with the passage of time and advances in technology. Astroturf, metal tennis rackets, high-powered rifles and instant-replay devices are only a few of the innovations that have made great changes in various sports. Astronauts have played golf on the moon. New sports such as sky diving have gained great popularity. And what of the future?

One thing is certain: human beings will always like to play games. It's as basic to our nature as curiosity, aggression, territoriality, or any of the other "primal urges" anthropologists like to tell us about. (Indeed, there's an anthropological theory that all human knowledge started with the proto-hominids' enjoyment of game-playing.)

But our world and our universe are growing larger every day, and new possibilities for sport will come with each year we move into the future. Will there one day be a solar regatta such as Arthur C. Clarke envisions in *Sunjammer*? How about playing football with super-strong aliens from a heavy-gravity planet, as in George R. R. Martin's *Run to Starlight*? Perhaps future gladiators will buy specially designed bodies to "wear" in the ring, or space prospectors will play polo amid the rings of Saturn, or bored humans on an alien planet will arrange to race the grotesque six-legged beasts of that world (see *The Body Builders, Mr. Meek Plays Polo,* and *The Great Kladnar Race*).

Poul Anderson and Gordon Dickson envision a future baseball game for the Galactic Pennant in which the teams look like teddy bears and octopi . . . and Malcolm Jameson has dreamed up an entirely new sport called Dazzle Dart.

Farfetched, "crazy" ideas? Maybe—but science fiction is a kind of game too, in which the skills are the authors' ability to imagine new possibilities and tell exciting stories about them. And the object of the science-fiction game is the same as that for any other—to have fun.

So get ready for a good time in the greatest sports arena of all, the future. Have a hot dog, cheer your favorites, and skip back a page or two if you want an instant replay.

                                                                    —Terry Carr

ANDERSON AND DICKSON

Poul Anderson and Gordon Dickson have been close friends since their days as undergraduates at the University of Minnesota thirty years ago. Both have had prolific and acclaimed careers writing science fiction; each has his shelf of Hugo and Nebula awards, and each has served as president of the Science Fiction Writers of America. But fans of both writers have a special fondness for the stories they've written together, especially their series of tales about the misadventures of the Hokas of Toka, alien beings who look like teddy bears and love everything about Earth's culture . . . so much so that they're constantly trying to imitate humans.

Here, in a story that's never before been reprinted, the Hokas pursue the delights of baseball with their usual enthusiasm—and some *very* unusual results.

Joy in Mudville

"Pla-a-a-ay *ball!*"

The long cry echoed through the park as Alexander Jones, plenipotentiary of the Interbeing League to the planet Toka, came through the bleacher entrance. Out on the field the pitcher wound up in a furry whirl of arms and legs and let go. Somehow the batter managed to shift his toothpick, grip the bat, and make ready while the ball was streaking at him. There was a clean crisp *smack* and the ball disappeared. The batter selected a fresh toothpick, stuck it in his mouth, jammed his hands in his pockets, and started a leisurely stroll around the diamond.

Alexander Jones was not watching this. He had heard the crack of the bat and seen the ball vanish; but following that there had been only a vague impression of something that roared by him and smashed into the bench above in a shower of splinters. As a former Interstellar Survey man, Alex was *ex officio* a reservist in the Solar Guard, and the promptness and decisiveness with which he hit the dirt now would have brought tears of fond pride to the eyes of his superior officers had they been there to see it.

However, they were not, and after holding his position for several seconds, Alex lifted a cautious head. Nobody else was up to bat; it looked safe to rise. He dusted himself off while glancing over the field.

It was spotted with small round forms, tubby, golden-furred, ursine-faced, the Hoka natives of the planet Toka. They were all in uniform, the outfit of long red underwear, short-sleeved shirts, loose abbreviated trousers, and peaked caps, which had been traditional for baseball since it was invented back on Earth. Even if most of the races throughout the known Galaxy which now played the game were not even remotely human, they all wore some variation of the costume. Alexander Jones often wondered if his kind might not, in the long run, go down in history less as the originators of space travel and the present leaders of the Interbeing League than as the creators of baseball.

Mighty Casey, the planet's star batter, had completed his home run—or home saunter—and returned to the benches. Lefty was warming up before he tried himself against The Babe. Professor, the intellectual outfielder, was at his post, keeping one eye on the diamond while the other studied a biography of the legendary George Herman Ruth. Beyond the bleachers, the high tile roofs of Mixumaxu lifted into a sunny sky. The Teddies were practicing, the day was warm, the lark on the wing, the snail on the thorn.

Putzy, the manager of the team, trotted worriedly up to Alex. He had been called something like Wishtu before the craze reached his planet; but the Hokas, perhaps the most adaptable race in the universe, the most enthusiastic innovators, had taken over names, language—everything!—from their human idols. Though of course they tended to be too literal-minded. . . .

"Ya all right?" he demanded. He had carefully cultivated hoarseness into his squeaky voice. "Ya didn't get a concussion or nuttin'?"

"I don't think so," answered Alex a little shakily. "What happened?"

"Ah, it wuz just mighty Casey," said Putzy. "We allus try a new pitcher out on him. Shows him he's gotta woik when he's up wit' duh Teddies."

"Er—yes," said Alex, mopping his brow. "He isn't going to hit any more this way, is he?"

"He knocks dat kind every time," said Putzy with pardonable smugness.

"*Every* time?" retorted Alex maliciously. "Did you ever hear the original poem of 'Casey at the Bat'?"

Putzy leaped forward, clapped a furry hand to Alex's mouth, and warned in a shaking whisper: "Don't never say dat! Geez, boss, ya don't know what duh sound of dat pome does to Casey. He ain't never got over dat day in Mudville!"

Alex winced. He might have known it. The Hoka mind was about as *sui generis* as a mind can get: quick, intelligent, eager, but so imaginative that it could hardly distinguish between fact and fiction and rarely bothered. Remembering other facets of Hoka-assimilated Earth culture—the Wild West, the Space Patrol, Sherlock Holmes, the Spanish Main, *la Légion Étrangère*—Alex might have known that the one who had adopted the role of mighty Casey would get so hypnotized by it as to start believing the ballad had happened to him personally.

"Never mind," he said. "I came over to get you. The Sarennians just arrived at the spaceport and their manager's due at my office in half an hour. I want you there to meet him."

"Okay," said Putzy, sticking an enormous cigar into his mouth. Alex shuddered as he lit up; tobacco grown on Toka gets strong enough to walk. They strolled out together, the pudgy little Hoka barely reaching the waist of the lean young human. Alex's runabout was waiting; it swung them above the walled city toward the flashy new skyscraper of the League Mission.

Seen from above, the town was a curious blend of the ancient and the ultramodern. As a technologically backward race, the Hokas were supposed to be introduced gradually to Galactic civilization; until they had developed so far, they were to be gently guarded from harming themselves or being harmed by any of the more advanced peoples. Alex, as League plenipotentiary, had the job of guide and guardian. It paid well and was quite a distinction; but he sometimes wondered if it wasn't making him old before his time. If the Hokas were just a little less individualistic and unpredictable . . .

The runabout set itself down on a landing flange of the skyscraper and Alex led the way inside. Ella, his native secretary, nodded at him from an electrowriter. There was a cigaret in her lipsticked mouth, but the effect of her tight blouse was somewhat spoiled for him by the fact that Hokas have twice the lactational equipment of humans. She was competent, but her last job had been with Mixumaxu's leading private eye.

Entering the inner office with Putzy, Alex flopped into a chair and put his feet on the desk. "Sit down," he invited. "Now look, before the Sarennian manager comes, I want to have a serious talk with you. It's about financing the team."

"We're doing okay," said Putzy, chewing on his cigar.

"Yes," said Alex grimly. "I know all about that. Your arrangement with these self-appointed outlaws in the so-called Sherwood Forest."

"It's fair enough," said Putzy. "Dey all get free passes."

"Nevertheless," said Alex after gulping for air, "things have got to be put on a more regular basis. Earth Headquarters likes the idea of you . . . people playing ball, it's a good way to get you accustomed to meeting other races, but I'm responsible for your accounts. Now I have a plan which is a little irregular, but I do have discretionary powers." He reached for some papers. "As you know, there are valuable uranium deposits on this planet which are being held in trust for your people; they're being robot-mined, and the proceeds have been going into the general planetary development fund. But there are enough other sources of income for that, so I've decided to divert the uranium mines to the Teddies' use. That will give you an income out of which to pay for necessities"—he paused and frowned—"and that does not include toothpicks for Casey!"

"But he's gotta have toot'picks!" cried the manager, shocked. "How kin he waggle a toot'pick without—"

"He can buy his own," said Alex sternly. "Salaries are paid to the team, you know. The same goes for that bookworm outfielder of yours, Professor—let him pay for his own books if he must read while he plays."

"Okay, okay. But we gotta have a likker fund. Duh boys gotta have deir snort."

Alex gave in on that. The fieriness of the Hoka distillation and the capacity of its creators were a Galactic legend. "All right. Sign here, Putzy. Under the law, native property has to be in native hands, so this gives you title to those mines, with the right to receive income from them and dispose of it as you see fit. Sometime next week I'll show you how to keep books."

The manager scrawled his name as Ella stuck her head in the door. She never would use the office annunciator. "A monster to see you, Chief," she said in a loud whisper.

"Ask him to wait a minute, will you?" said Alex. He turned to Putzy. "Now look, please be as polite as you can when the Sarennian comes in. I don't want any trouble."

"What's duh lowdown on dem, anyway?" inquired Putzy. "All I know is we play 'em here next mont' for duh Sector pennant."

"They—well, I don't know." Alex coughed. "Just between us, I don't like them much. It isn't their appearance, of course; I've been friends with weirder beings than they are. It's something in their culture, something ruthless. . . . They're highly civilized, full members of the League and so on, but it's all that the rest of the planets can do to restrain their expansionism. By hook or by crook, they want to take over the leadership." He brightened. "Oh, well, we're only going to play ball with them."

"*Only!*" cried Putzy, aghast. "What's so only about it? Man, dis is for duh Sector pennant. Dis ain't no bush-league braggle. Dis is a crooshul series!"

Alex shrugged. "All right, so it is." But he could sympathize with his charges. The Hokas had come far and fast in a mere ten years. It would mean a lot to them to win Sector championship.

The Galactic Series necessarily operated under some rather special rules. In a civilization embracing thousands of stars and still expanding, one year just wasn't enough to settle a tournament. The Series had been going on for more than two centuries now. On the planets local teams contended in the sub-series for regional championships; regions fought it out for continental victories, and continents settled the planetary supremacy. Then there were whole systems, and series between systems, all going on simultaneously. . . . Alex's brain reeled at the thought.

Extrapolating present expansion of the League frontiers, sociologists estimated that the play-off for the Galactic Pennant would occur in about 500 years. It looked very much as if the Toka Teddies might be in the running then. In one short decade, their energy and enthusiasm had made them ready to play Sarenn for the Sector pennant. The sector embraced a good thousand stars, but Toka had bypassed most of these by defeating previously established multistellar champions.

"If we lose," said Putzy gloomily, "back to duh bush leagues for anudder ten-twen'y years, and mebbe we'll never get a chanst at duh big game." He cheered up. "Ah, who's worrying? Casey ain't been struck out yet, and Lefty got a coive pitch dat's outta dis univoise."

Alex pressed a button and spoke into the annunciator. "Send the gentlebeing in, Ella." He rose politely; after all, Ush Karuza, manager of the Sarenn Snakes, *was* a sort of ambassador.

The monster squished in. He stood well over two meters high, on long, clawed legs; half a dozen ropy tentacles ending in strong boneless fingers circled his darkly gleaming body under the ridged, blubbery-faced head. Bulging eyes regarded Alex with a cold, speculative stare, but he bowed courteously enough. "Your servant, sir," he murmured in tolerably good English.

"Welcome . . . ah . . . Mr. Karuza," said Alex. "May I introduce Putzy Ballswatter, the manager of the Teddies? Won't you sit down?"

Putzy rose and the two beings nodded distantly at each other. Ush Karuza sniffed and unfolded a trapezelike arrangement he was carrying. When he had draped himself over this, he lay waiting.

"Well," said Alex, swinging into the little speech he had prepared, "I'm sure you two will get along famously—"

Putzy, who had been staring at Ush Karuza, muttered something to himself.

"Did you say something, Putzy?" asked Alex.

"Nuts!" said Putzy.

"Hiss!" hissed the Sarennian.

"Well, as I was saying," continued Alex hurriedly, "you'll get along famously as you ready yourselves for the big contest—"

Putzy seemed on the verge of speaking again.

"—in your *separate* training camps," went on Alex loudly, "at *good* distances from each other—" Under the rules, a team playing off its own world had to have a month's training on the other planet to accustom itself to the new conditions. There was

also a handicapping system so complicated that no human brain
could master it.

Alex knew what the trouble was this time. It was something
he had kept carefully to himself since first learning that the
Teddies were to play the Snakes. The fact was that the Sarennians bore a slight but unfortunate resemblance to the Slissii, the
reptile race which had been the Hokas' chief rival for control of
Toka from time immemorial till men arrived to help out; and the
fur on the little manager's neck had risen visibly at the mere
sight of his opposite number.

What was worse, Ush Karuza seemed to be experiencing a
like reaction toward Putzy. Even as Alex watched, the tentacled
monster produced a small bottle which he opened and wafted
gently before his nose like a disdainful dandy of the Louis
Quinze period on Earth. For a second, Alex merely blinked, and
then a whiff from the bottle reached his own nostrils. He gagged.

Putzy's sensitive nose was wrinkling too. Ush Karuza came
as close to smirking as a being with fangs in its mouth could.

"Ah . . . merely a little butyl mercaptan, ssirss," he hissed.
"Our atmosphere contains a ssimilar compound. It iss necessary
to our metabolissm. Quite harmless to man and Hoka."

"Um . . . ugh . . . ah?" said Alex brightly. Out of the corner
of his eye he saw Putzy grind out his dead cigar in the ashtray
and dig another one twice the size out of his baggy uniform shirt.
He fired it up. Butyl mercaptan sallied forth to meet and mingle
with blue noisome clouds of smoke.

"Ah, ssso!" mumbled Karuza furiously and began to waft
his bottle more energetically.

Puff! Puff! Puff! went Putzy.

"Gentlebeings, gentlebeings, please!" wheezed Alex, taking the heavy paperweight away from Putzy.

Venomously hissing, Ush Karuza was uncorking a second
bottle while Putzy crammed more cigars into his mouth.

Things were off to a fine start.

Alexander Jones came staggering home to his official resi-
dence that night in a mood to be comforted by his beautiful
blond wife, Tanni. But the house was empty, she having taken

the children for a few days to the Hoka Bermuda for its annual sack by pirates (a notable social event on Toka), and dinner was served by the Admirable Crichton with his usual nerve-racking ostentation. It was only afterward, sitting alone in the study with a Scotch and soda, that Alex's ganglia stopped vibrating.

The study was a comfortable book-lined room with a cheerful fire, and when he had slipped into a dressing gown and placed himself before the desk, Alex realized that privacy was just what he needed. He pressed the door-lock button, opened a secret drawer, and got out a sheaf of papers.

Let not the finger of scorn be pointed at Alexander Jones. The most amiable, conscientious, thoroughly normal young men still have their hidden vices; perhaps these outlets are what keep them on their orbits, and surely Alex had more troubles than most who shoulder the Earthman's burden. What the universe needs is more candor, more tolerance and understanding of human weakness. The truth is that Alexander Jones was a poet.

Like most great creative artists, he was frustrated by the paradoxes of public taste. As a Solar Guardsman, he had achieved immortality by his poetic gifts. It was he who had originated the limerick about the spaceman and girl in free fall, as well as the "Ballad of the Transparent Spacesuits," and these shall live forever. Yet they were merely the sparks of his careless youth and he now winced to recall them. His spirit was with the Avantist Revival; his idols had never been known outside of a select clique: Rimbaud, Baudelaire, cummings, Eliot, Cogswell. From time to time the interstellar mails carried manuscripts signed "J. Alexander" to the offices of *microcosm: the minuscule magazine*. So far, they had also carried the manuscripts back. But a shoulderer of the Earthman's burden is not easily discouraged.

Alex took a long drink, placed stylus to paper, and began writing:

> *the circumambient snake surrounds the palpitating*
> *tarry fever-dream of uncertain distortions and Siva*
> *screams and mutters unheard vacillations: now? then?*
> *Perhaps later, it is hot today.–*

The visio set interrupted him with a buzz. He swore and pressed the *Accept* button. The features of a rather woozy-looking Hoka appeard on the screen.

"Hi-yah, bosh," said the apparition.

"Putzy!" cried Alex. "You're drunk!"

"I am not," Putzy replied indignantly, momentarily reeling out of screen range. "Shober as a judge," he said, reappearing. "Coupla liters ish all I had. Wouldn't make a pup drunk. It's dis yer stuff Ush Karuza smokes when he's shelebratin'. Dese Sarennians don' drink. Dey just smokes uh stuff. Makes me kinda light-headed—smellin' it—" Putzy went over backwards.

Climbing back into view, he said with heavy gravity: "I called y'up t' tell ya shumfin. You said be nice to Karuza, di'n' ya?"

"Yes," said Alex, a dreadful premonition seizing him.

"Thash what I thought ya said. Well, listen. Like yuh said, we wen' out for li'l drink. Had li'l talk, like yuh said we should. We got t' talkin' shop, shee, an' I tol' him 'bout dose uranium mine rights. Right away he wan'ed ta bet me some salt mines on Sarenn against 'em. So I did."

"You did?" yelped Alex.

"Sure I did. Signed duh papers an' all. Di'n ya say be nice to him? But listen—" Putzy beckoned mysteriously and Alex leaned forward, shaking. Putzy went on in a whisper. "Here's duh t'ing. Not on'y has I made him happy, but we got us some salt mines."

"How come?" moaned Alex.

"Because!" said Putzy strongly, driving his point home with a stubby finger jabbed into the screen before him. "Because he don' know it yet, but duh Teddies is gonna win."

"Is that so?" barked Alex.

"Sure, an' yuh know why?"

Alex shook his head numbly. "No, why?"

"Because," said Putzy triumphantly, "duh Snakes is gonna lose."

He beamed. "Jush t'ought ya'd like to know, bosh. So long."

"Hey!" screamed Alex. "Come back here!"

He was too late. The screen was blank.

"Oh, *no!*" he gasped. "Not this!"

For a wild instant, his only thought was of *quotation at the waterfront*. It had been shaping up so nicely! Wouldn't he ever get a chance to write something really significant?

Then he settled back to realities and wished he hadn't.

Tottering to his office the next morning after a sleepless night, he took an athetrine tablet and called the Mission library to send up Volume GAK-GAR of *Basic Interstellar Law*. When he received it, he turned to the section on gambling between things from different planets. He had to find out if the bet Putzy had made with Karuza could be legally collected or not. The legislation in question turned out to be full of such witty statements as, "The above shall apply in all cases covered by Smith *vs*. Xputui except in such cases as are covered by Sections XCI through CXXIII inclusive"—each of these with its own quota of exceptions and references. After two hours, he was still no closer to an answer.

He sighed, sent Ella out for more coffee, and was just settling down to a fresh assault on the problem when there was a sort of swirl in the air before him and a semi-humanoid specimen with an enormous bald head topping a spindly little body materialized in his visitor's chair.

"Greetings, youth!" boomed the newcomer. "My visualization of the cosmic all implies that you are surprised. Do not be so. Be advised that I am Nicor of Rishana, who is to umpire the forthcoming contest between Toka and Sarenn."

Alex recovered from his astonishment. The Rishanans, the most intellectual race in the known Galaxy, were almost legends. They could be lured from their home only by a problem impossible for lesser races to solve. Such was any game governed by the twenty seven huge volumes of the Interstellar Baseball Association rules; as a result, Rishanans invariably officiated in the Series as umpires.

Otherwise they ignored the rest of the Galaxy and were ignored by it. Undoubtedly they had a lot on the ball—for instance, whatever tiny machine or inborn psionic ability permitted them to project themselves through space at will; but since nobody really misses the brains he doesn't have, the rest of the

League had never fallen prey to any sort of inferiority complex. Indeed, most beings felt rather sorry for the poor dwarfs. Since the Rishanans felt rather sorry for the poor morons, everybody was happy.

Inspiration came to Alex. "May I ask you a question, sir?" he begged.

"Of course you may ask a question," snapped Nicor. "Any ego may ask a question. What you really wish to know is whether I will answer the question." He paused and looked uncertain. "Or have you already asked me the question? Time is a variable, you know."

"No, I didn't know," said Alex politely.

"Yes, indeed," thundered the voice of that incredible ancient being. "As determined by Sonrak's hypothesis. But come, come, youth—the question."

"Oh, er, yes." Alex pointed to the law book. I'm having a little trouble with a small point here. Just a—heh! heh!—a theoretical question, you know, sir. If a Hoka bet a Sarennian some Tokan land, and lost, could the—er—say the Sarennian collect?"

"Certainly," snapped Nicor. "That is, he would collect by respective substitute."

"I beg your pardon?"

"You need not apologize for inferior mentality. In effect, the Hokas, being wards of the League, would be protected; but as plenipotentiary and responsible individual, you would have to pay the winner an equivalent amount."

"What?" cried Alex as the assessed valuation of the uranium mines—a fourteen-digit figure—reeled before him.

He heard the explanation through a blur. The extreme libertarians who had drawn up the League Constitution had protected ordinary citizens right and left but deliberately placed high officials on a limb. In this case, a judgment in equity would send him to the Sarennian salt mines for—oh, in view of the new longevity techniques, about fifty years, turning his wages over to Ush Karuza. The working conditions were not too bad unless one happened to have a distaste for the odor of the mercaptans.

"—well, well, enough of this pleasant but unprofitable

chitchat, youth," finished Nicor. "Let us be off to the ball game."

"What game?" asked Alex weakly. "The pennant game isn't for another month."

"Tut-tut," reproved Nicor. "Don't interrupt. I am, of course, both forgiving and gracious. Perhaps you think an intellectual like myself has no sense of humor. So many beings fall into the misapprehension. Certainly I have a sense of humor. Of course, it is more subtle than yours; and naturally I am not amused by the crude horseplay of lesser intelligences. In fact," went on Nicor, his brow darkening, "that is the main trouble with beings of small development. They do not take the cosmic all seriously enough. No dignity, youth, no dignity."

"But wait a minute—" broke in Alex.

"Don't interrupt! As an intelligence of the quaternary class, you cannot possibly make an interruption of sufficient importance to interfere with a statement emanating from an intelligence of my class. As I was saying . . . dignity. Dignity! That is what is so painfully lacking in the younger races." A thundercloud gathered on his face. "When I think of the presumption of those few rash individuals who have dared to question my—MY!—decisions upon the baseball field— But I am sure your charges will be guilty of no such indiscretion."

Alex rocked in his chair. If there was any sport the Hokas loved with a pure and undying love, it was umpire-baiting.

"As for your quaint belief that this is not the day of the game," continued Nicor, "I could hardly expect you to know. You irresponsible children never know. When I was your age, I used to have to get up every morning and figure time as a variable to fourteen decimal places before I could start my day's calculations. We didn't have Sonraks in those days to help us. The trouble with you present youths is that you have it too easy. Surely you do not think I would put myself in the ridiculous position of having to realign myself for thirty days in the future? Naturally, I devoted only one point eight percent of my reasoning power to this business of establishing my spatio-temporal coordinates, but it is inconceivable that I should fail. No, no, rest assured that this is the day of the game."

Alex pointed a mute finger at the chronopiece on the wall. Nicor whirled and stared at it.

"What?" he roared with a volume that shook the office. "Am I to be given the lie by a mechanical? Am I to be outfaced by a planet? Am I to be maladjusted by a cosmic integral of the square root of minus one over log log tangent X, theta R squared over N, dx, from zero to infinity? Blast Sonrak! Damn the misplaced decimal point! Time is *not* a variable!"

And with an explosion that rocked the room, he vanished.

Now, it seemed, everything depended on the Teddies' winning the game. Alex visited the Hoka ball park and tried to make Putzy institute more rigorous training. The Hokan idea of practice was to let Casey swat a few wild ones while the basemen and fielders sat down, puffing cigars, tilting jugs to their lips, and chatting lightly of this and that. To Alex's protests that the Snakes were bound to get some hits when they came up to bat, Putzy reported that Lefty would fan them or, failing that, fielders with the speed of the Professor would easily tag them out. Alex gave up.

He made an excuse to drop in on the Sarennian training camp. The visitors were good, no denying that: their main advantage was their terrific tentacle spread, handy for nabbing flying balls; and when the pitcher was winding up, you couldn't see what kind of pitch was coming among all those arms, or even what arm it was coming from. But they lacked the Hoka swiftness and hitting power. Alex—who had spent long hours under a hypnoteacher cramming himself with baseball lore—decided that one set of advantages just about offset the other, so that there would be no handicapping.

Ush Karuza looked positively gloating under his superficial good manners, and Alex began to get suspicious. Considering the ambitions of Sarenn, there was probably more at stake than the pennant and a bet. Returning to his office, the man consulted the Service roster and found that a Sarennian was now at the top of the list of those waiting for ambassadorial vacancies and, if Toka's plenipotentiary were removed, would probably get the

job. Since Sarenn was fairly close to the Tokan sun while Earth
was far away, it wouldn't take long for the new chief to gain
complete control of the planet for his people without attracting
too much attention at Headquarters.

And a plenipotentiary sent to the salt mines would naturally not retain his position.

Alex looked hollowly into space. He didn't even have Tanni
to comfort him; she had messaged an intention to stay on awhile
in Bermuda and he had agreed, not wishing to torment her with
worry that might turn out to be needless. His carefully guided
planet was headed for tyrannous foreign rule; he was headed for
the same; *microcosm* had just returned *Greeks en Brochette*. . . .

There is an old saying that "the optimist declares this is the
best of all possible worlds; the pessimist is afraid he's right."
Alex agreed.

The big day dawned bright and clear and hot. Since early
morning, a colorful throng of Hokas had been flocking into the
ball park. They had come not only from Mixumaxu and its
neighboring city-states, but reflected the varied impact of
human culture on their entire planet. A booted and spurred
cowboy sat next to a top-hatted Victorian gentleman; a knight in
armor clanked past a tubby Space Patrolman; a sashed character
with a skull and crossbones on his cocked hat grumbled saltily,
"Scupper my mizzenmast!" as he tripped on his cutlass. One
part of the stands was reserved for Sarennian spectators, a silent
and impassive mass of tentacles.

As Alex walked across the field to his official seat in the
Hoka dugout, he scowled. The substitutes were all present and
accounted for, but where was the regular team?

"Hot dogs, pop cawn, soda pop!" bawled a vendor in the
stands above. "Getcha pop here, folks. Can't kill duh umpire
wit'out a pop bottle!"

Alex's worried eyes traveled across the dusty ground to the
center of the infield. Nicor of Rishana was already there, leaning
on the bookcase containing the twenty-seven volumes of rules.
There was a grim look on his face which might have been caused
by thoughts of Sonrak, and a slightly withdrawn expression in

his eyes as he mentally scanned the field from all necessary points of view. This psionic ability had enabled the number of umpires to be reduced to one, even as the easy exhaustion of some races had forced changes in the rules governing substitutions.

"Where's our team?" muttered Alex. "They're late already."

The buzz from the bleachers became a chant. "We want the Teddies. We want the Teddies. We want the Teddies."

Then there was a ragged cheer as the famous nine came into sight—not from the locker room, but from the main gate. Even at that distance, Alex saw how they staggered. Leading the way was Ush Karuza, looking smug and supporting Putzy, who was singing something about somebody called Adeline. Alex broke into a cold sweat.

Putzy lurched up to him while the rest of the team was calling cheery greetings to their friends in the stands and forcing autographed balls on them. "Hi-yah," burbled the Hoka manager, collapsing into Alex's arms. "I gotta tell ya shumfin. We got dese Sarennians all wrong. Good ol' Ush, he's all right. Ya know what he done? He took us all out dis mornin' an' stood us to duh bigges' dinner in town. All duh steak an' French fries we could eat. Whoops!" He lost his grip and sat down suddenly. "T'ink I'll take a li'l nap." His beady eyes closed.

Alex glared at the Snake manager. "Is this your idea of fair play?" he asked. "Drugging our team. Umpire!"

Nicor flickered in midair and appeared beside them. "What is it, youth?"

"This—" Alex pointed shakily at Ush Karuza. "This gentlebeing took our men out and drugged them with that stuff he smokes."

"My dear ssir!" protested the monster. "It iss merely a mild sstimulant that we Ssarennianss ssmoke for pleasure I am not accountable if it affectss our little friendss."

Alex opened his mouth indignantly. "Down, youth!" snapped Nicor. "There is nothing in the rules covering pre-game festivities." He returned to midfield.

Another Sarennian pushed forward a great wheeled tank.

"Ice cream," announced Ush Karuza grandly. "Help yoursselvess, my friendss!" As the Hokas threw themselves on it with besotted cries of glee, he pulled a book out of his pouch and gave it to the Professor. "And for you," he added, "a brand-new biography of Tyruss Cobb, sspecially prepared by the Ssarennian Sstate Department."

"Oh, boy!" The small, bespectacled Hoka sat down and began reading it at once. Ush Karuza oozed off with every appearance of satisfaction. Alex buried his face in his hands.

Nicor of Rishana spoke into his wrist microphone, and his voice boomed over the park: "Come, youths! My visualization demands that you now play ball!"

The spectators cheered. The band, somewhat confused, broke into "Auld Lang Syne." The Toka Teddies wobbled out onto the field. Putzy sat up and muttered something about not feeling so good.

The Snakes, as visitors, were first up to bat. Their star hitter, Shimpur Sumis, wrapped his tentacles around his club and waved it gleefully. Lefty, the Teddy pitcher, found his way to the mound and began turning around to get his position. He kept on turning.

"Play ball, youth!" thundered the umpire. Shimpur Sumis yawned.

It seemed to infuriate Lefty. He sent his ball spinning in faster than Alex could follow. Either because he wasn't quite himself, or because he hadn't allowed for the greater reach of Sarennian tentacles, Shimpur Sumis connected with a solid hit. The ball smacked into left field. The monster dropped his bat and galumphed toward first base.

"Grab it, Professor!" screamed Alex.

The intellectual outfielder was too immersed in his new book to notice. The ball shot past him. His fans howled, "Wake up, ya bum! Grab dat ball!"

Shimpur Sumis rounded second.

A Hoka near Alex, clad in doublet and hose and feathered cap, leaped up, fitted an arrow to his longbow, and let fly. The Professor yelled as it pinked him, glared around, saw the ball, and loped after it. By a miracle, he got it back to the catcher just as Sumis went by third. The Sarennian retreated, grinning smugly.

The next one stepped up to bat. Lefty sent a whizzer past him. The ball smacked into the catcher's mitt.

"Ball one!" cried Nicor.

"Whaddaya mean, ball one?" squeaked Lefty, spinning around in a rage. "Dat wuz a strike if I ever seen one."

"A strike," said Nicor, glowering, "must pass between waist and shoulders."

"Yeah, but he ain't got any waist or any shoulders," protested Lefty.

"Hmmm, yes, so I see." Nicor pulled one of the fat volumes out of the bookcase beside him and consulted it. Then he took forth a transit and sighted on the batter. The crowd rumbled impatiently.

"The equivalent median line," said Nicor at last, "yields the incontrovertible result that the missile so injudiciously aimed was, indeed, ball one."

Alex shuddered. Putzy turned green under his fur.

The next ball met a hard-swinging bat. Again it zoomed by the immersed Professor. Again the archer fired. This time the Professor was ready. He plucked the arrow out of the air as it neared him and continued reading. Both Sarennians loped home. Their rooters set up a football-style cheer:

> Hiss, hiss, hiss!
> Who iss better than thiss?
> Squirmy worm, destiny's germ—
> TEAM!!!

The next Sarennian went out on a pop fly just behind third. The one after that made it to first. But Lefty, even when pitching on hope and instinct, was not a hurler to be despised. The fifth Sarennian up to bat barely got a piece of the ball and both he and the Snake on base were put out in a wobbly double play.

The Teddies came to bat. They were uniformly ineffective with the single exception of mighty Casey, who, as Putzy was too sick to tell him not to, tried to fulfill a long-standing ambition to lay down a bunt, but only succeeded in bunting the ball over the left-field fence. Score one run for the Teddies.

The next four innings were a rout. The regular Teddy team got even sicker and had to be taken out, and against the substitutes, the Sarennians made blissful scores. At the end of the first half of the fifth inning, the board read 7 to 1 in favor of the Snakes.

By the second half of the fifth, the original team members were weak but recovered, and ready to take the field again with blood in their eyes. Casey was first up, and with a valiant return to his usual nonchalance, he put his hands in his pockets and sauntered toward the plate, a toothpick in his mouth and scorn in his eye. He whipped into his batting stance just as the Sarennian pitcher let go. There was a blur, a crack, and he was strolling off along the baseline, nodding graciously to his fans.

But for him it had been a poor and a weak hit. The Sarennian left fielder reached forth an interminable tentacle and nabbed it as it came smoking along the ground. He whirled and shot it back toward first base. Casey saw it coming and broke into a panting run. He thundered into first together with the ball.

"Out!" said Nicor, appearing at the bag.

"Out???" screamed Casey, skidding to a stop and coming back. "I wuz in dere ahead o' duh ball wit' enough time fer a nap."

"I say out," ruled Nicor. "Do not dispute with a superbrain— Time! Don't mention that word time to me!"

"Why, ya blind, bloody, concrete-skulled superbrain!"

Pop bottles began to fly from the stands, bursting to fragments in the air as the small robot-controlled anti-aircraft guns mounted on the right-field fence went into action. Nicor ignored the bombardment and settled the discussion by flickering back into position behind the pitcher's mound.

The game continued. The Teddies were still a little weak and uncertain. The Hoka following Casey was caught out at shortstop and the next Hoka sent a high fly into right field, where it was easily taken for the putout.

The Snakes came up to bat in the first half of the sixth inning. Lefty, turned white-hot with determination, retired the opposing side without gain by three straight strikeouts. The Hokas took over at the plate and the first six men up scored two men and loaded the bases. The score stood at 7 to 3 with Casey yet to bat, and the Snakes called time out.

"What is the occasion, youth?" demanded Nicor of Ush Karuza.

The Sarennian smirked. "I find I musst invoke one of the handicapping ruless, ssir," he answered. "Article Forty-Three, SSection Three, Paragraph Twenty-two-*b*. In effect, it iss that a certain gass is necessary to our playerss'ss metabolissm. It being a mercaptan, completely non-toxic in small dosess, ass you know, we may ssimply releasse it without sslowing the game down by wearing masskss and handicapping the Hokass."

"There are psychosomatic effects," objected Nicor. "I refer to the nauseous stench involved."

"I do not believe the ruless ssay anything about ssuch sside issuess," answered Karuza smugly.

Nicor went back to the books. At last he nodded. "I fear you are right," he agreed sadly. "But in the name of sportsman-ship—"

Ush Karuza turned purple with rage and swelled up alarm-ingly. "Sssir! How dare you!" he hissed. "Article Two Hundred Thirty-Two, Amendment Number Five Hundred Fifty-Ssix, Paragraph Three-*a*, explissitly sstatess that Ssarennianss are incapable of the conssept of Ssportssmanship and sspessifically exemptss them from obsserving it."

"Oh." Nicor looked crestfallen. He checked. "True," he said bitterly.

Alex felt ill already. This looked like the end.

A great generator was wheeled into an upwind position on the field. It began to fume. Alex caught a whiff and felt his stomach rise in revolt. There could only be a few parts per million in the air, but it was enough!

"Oof!" groaned Putzy beside him. "Lemme outta here."

"You stay," said Alex desperately, grabbing him. "Play up, play up, and play the game!"

Nicor turned a delicate green. "My visualization of the cosmic all suggests I am going to be sick," he muttered.

Putzy opened a box of cigars and passed them around to his team. "Dis may help ya fer a little while," he said. "Now get in dere and fight!" Tears rose in his eyes. "Me aged grandmudder is sitting at home, boys, old and sick, laying dere amongst her roses and lavender waiting for yuh to bring home duh pennant. It'll kill duh sweet old lady if ya lose—"

"Ah shaddap!" said his grandmother, leaning out of her place in the stands beside him and stuffing her knitting in his mouth.

Alex fumed away on his own cigaret, trying to drown the smell that curled around him. There must be some way to escape those salt mines!

With the mercaptan turning his stomach upside down on top of the effects of the drug, Casey still batted in the man on third on a sacrifice fly. The Hoka following him struck out. Retired, the Teddies lurched out onto the field and took another pasting. The score climbed against them—six Sarenn runs in the seventh, seven in the eighth, with the brief one-two-three interlude of the Teddies at bat hardly noticeable in the Snakes' slugging festival. When the Hokas came up again in the bottom of the eighth, they were trailing 20 to 4.

Alex chewed his fingernails. There must be an answer to this! There must be some counterirritant, something that would get the Hokas back to the careless energy and childlike enthusiasm which served them so well. . . . Counteragents! The idea flared in his head.

He snatched at the water boy's arm. "Bring us something to drink!" he commanded. The little ursinoid sped away, to return with a slopping bucket which Alex knew very well did not contain water.

"Time out!" he yelled. "The Hokas request time out."

"What for, youth?" asked Nicor faintly.

"They need alcohol to protect themselves against the effects of the Sarennian gas. It's okay by the rule books, I'm sure."

Nicor brighted a little. "It does protect?" he inquired. "Then, youth, you may bring me some too."

Ush Karuza jittered about in a rage while the Teddies gathered weakly around the bucket and dipped their noses into it. Even by Hoka standards, they got it down fast. Nicor scowled at his complimentary beaker, sipped, winced, and gasped. "*This is necessary to them?*" he cried. "I have seen halogen breathers, I have seen energy eaters, I have seen drinkers of molten lead, but here is the race that shall rule the sevagram!"

Casey lifted his dripping black snout. "Urp," he said. "Gotta toot'pick?"

"Play ball!" hollered Ush Karuza wrathfully.

The Babe waved casually at Putzy. "We'll get 'em," he said confidently, and connected with the first pitch for a clean single to left. The Professor came up with his book in one hand, stuck it under his arm just long enough to belt one out of the park, and walked home with his nose back in his book.

"Geez!" he muttered reverently. "Dat Cobb could sure play *ball!*"

Lefty stepped up to bat with an evil gleam in his eye. The Sarennian star pitcher launched a ferocious fast ball across the middle. Lefty let it go by. "Ooooof!" said the catcher.

"Strike one," said Nicor.

Time out to replace one catcher.

There was no second strike. Lefty bounced the next pitch off the right-field wall for a stand-up triple.

Casey sneered and sauntered out to the plate. Grabbing the end of the Sarennian catcher's fourth tentacle, he began picking his teeth with it.

"Halt! Stop! Foul!" shrieked Karuza. "He *bit* my player!"

Some of Alex's hard-won baseball knowledge came to his aid. "Article Forty-One, Section Five, Paragraph Seventeen-*a*: 'Players may take such nourishment as is required during the game,' " he flung back.

"But not off *my* players!" wailed Karuza.

Nicor weaved over to his books and consulted them. "I am afraid I can find nothing forbidding cannibalism," he announced. "It must never have occurred to the commission. Tsk, tsk."

The pitcher let fly. Casey set his bat end-on on the plate and jumped up to balance on top of it. "Strike one!" called Nicor.

"Nope," said Casey owlishly. "Yuh mean ball one, ump.

Duh ball went under m' waist. Under m' feet, in fack!"

"So it did," agreed Nicor imperturbably. "Ball one!"

"The ruless—" sputtered Ush Karuza.

"Nothing in the rules against balancing on top of a bat, youth." Nicor scratched his bulging head. "I do believe the commission will have to call a special meeting after this game."

The Sarennian pitcher wound up again. As the ball zoomed toward him, Casey swung the mightiest swing in Toka's history. The Snakes' second baseman saw the ball screaming at him and dropped to the ground in terror. A bolder monster in the outfield raised his glove and caught it. Or perhaps one should say it caught him—he was lifted off the ground, described a beautiful arc, and landed three meters away. The ball went merrily on to cave in a section of the fence beyond.

Casey, who had been spinning on one heel unable to stop, came to a halt and staggered around the bases. He had plenty of time, because the Sarennians had to dig the ball out from between two planks.

Time out while the Snakes replaced one unconscious outfielder and one second baseman with a bad case of the shakes.

The rest of the Hokas followed the example of their star players and sailed twice completely through their lineup before being retired with a score of 19 to the Snakes' 20 at the end of the eighth. The crowd, including Alex, was going wild.

Shimpur Sumis came up to bat with a haughty look suggesting that he alone could settle the matter. Lefty, who was higher than a kite, threw him a ball so fast that it exploded on being struck. Nicor consulted his library for the rule on exploding balls, found none, and called it a strike ... though he admitted that his visualization was not very complete today. Sumis' abused tentacles could not handle the bat well enough to keep him from being struck out.

Ush Karuza snarled and went over to the mercaptan generator and opened the valves wide. A thick, nearly visible stream of vapor rolled across the field to envelop the Hoka pitcher.

Lefty was too drunk to care. He sent off his famous curve.

Then he gaped at it. So did the Snake batter. So did Alex. No—the ball couldn't possibly be where it was!

It landed in the catcher's mitt. "Strike one!" announced Nicor.

The next pitch was even more unbelievable than the last. It defied all known natural laws and went in a sine curve. "Strike two!"

The batter flailed wildly the third time. Alex distinctly saw the club go through the ball, but nothing happened.

"Strike three!" said Nicor. "Youth, you are now external to the n-dimensional sociological hypersphere!"

"Huh?" asked Putzy.

"He means, 'You're out,' " translated Alex happily.

"Foul!" bawled Ush Karuza. "They're using black magic."

"There is nothing in the rules against magic," said Nicor.

"I just t'row a damn good coive, dat's all," said Lefty belligerently.

The next Sarennian fared no better. By that time Alex had figured out the situation. "The thick stream of mercaptan vapor has a refractive index appreciably different from air," he told Putzy. "No wonder it produces optical illusions. Hoist by their own petard!"

Putzy seemed dubious. "If dat means what I t'ink it means," he said, "you shouldn't oughtta say it in front of me grandmudder."

The Teddies came to their their turn at bat. It was the last half of the ninth inning. The score stood at 19 to 20 with the Teddies trailing. The batting order at that moment stood: first The Babe, then the Professor, then Lefty, and then Casey. The Sarennians looked grim, but the Hokas in the stands, who had resorted to their potent pocket flasks while the team was getting its liquor from the water boy, were wildly jubilant. As The Babe picked up his bat and strode to the plate, they began a cheer which finally died away to an awful silence as the whole crowd held its breath.

The Sarennian pitcher was clearly determined to let no hits be gotten off him. He wound up and let fly.

From the stands rose a mighty groan of horror, interspersed

with shrill hoots of glee from the Sarennian section. For the stream of mercaptan vapor was still flowing past the pitcher *and all three balls weaved a daisy chain past the plate!*

"Strike three!" cried Nicor. "Out!"

Sadly, The Babe came back. The stands were in an uproar. It looked as if open battle might break out between the Hoka and Sarennian fans. Alex cringed on his bench.

The Professor went up to the plate. The ball looped crazily by him. "Strike one!"

A long moan of agony went up from the Hokas.

"Strike two!"

The Professor braced himself. There was a wild, almost berserk gleam in his spectacles. The Sarennian pitcher writhed and twirled his tentacles with contemptuous confidence. The ball shot forward.

The Professor threw himself and his bat to meet it.

There was a tiny *tick*. The ball popped out of the vapor fog and trickled along the ground toward third base. There were only a few seconds of time before it was caught, but that was all the Professor's famous legs needed. There was a whiz, a blur, an explosion of dust, and the Hoka was safe at first.

The tying run was on, and there were two outs left to bring it home.

Lefty took his time selecting his bat. He swung it heavily a few times to test the balance and then slowly stalked up to the plate. The pitcher wound up. He threw. The stands groaned.

"*Strike one!*" thundered Nicor in a voice of doom.

"Casey," said Putzy in a shaking tone, "get ready, boy."

Alex turned to look at the Teddies' mainstay. To his surpise, the little batter seemed cool and calm. "Relax, Putzy," Casey said. "It's in duh bag. All I gotta do is knock us bot' home."

"But dose pitches!" said Putzy.

"Lissen!" said Casey with some heat. "Lissen, ya don't t'ink I ever bodders to watch d' pitcher, do yuh? All I pays attention to is duh ball from duh time it gets to about two meters away from me. And duh ball gotta be straight den, or duh ump calls it a foul. Dey can't fool me none."

Slowly, hope began to dawn on Putzy's furry face. He was

even smiling as Nicor called "Strike three!" and Lefty returned glumly from the plate.

Casey got to his feet and began his customary nonchalant stroll toward the batter's box. At first the crowd merely gaped at him in astonishment; but then, drawing courage from his apparent confidence, they raised a swelling cheer that rocked the stands. He doffed his cap and kissed his hand to the fans, waved, rubbed his hands in the dirt, and took up his stance. Alex saw, through a vision blurred by tenseness, that the Sarennian pitcher was already losing heart at sight of this overweening opponent.

"Time out!" screamed Ush Karuza.

For a moment the park was held in agonized silence. Then a mounting growl like that of a Boomeringian sea-bear disturbed at its meal commenced and grew.

"For what reason, youth?" asked Nicor.

"Article Thirty-Six, Section Eight, Paragraph Nineteen-k," said Ush Karuza defiantly. "Any manager may encourage hiss team by verbal meanss."

Nicor checked. "Correct," he said. "You may proceed."

There was a scurry from the Sarennian dugout and a public-address system was wheeled onto the field and its microphone set up before a small tape player. As the stands waited silently to see what this new move might portend, Ush Karuza switched it on. There was a hissing noise as the machine warmed up.

At the plate, Casey smiled indulgently.

And then the hissing stopped and a voice boomed over the park. It was not a Sarennian voice, but human; and the first words it uttered wiped the smile from Casey's lips and fell on the field like the hand of doom. For the voice was reciting, and the first words were:

> It looked extremely rocky for the Mudville nine that
>   day:
> The score stood two to four with but one inning left to
>   play.
> So when Cooney died at second . . .

"Oh, no!" wailed Putzy. "It's *it*!"

"What's it?" choked Alex.

"Dat pome—'*Casey at duh Bat*'—oooh, lookit poor Casey now—" The manager pointed a trembling finger at the Teddies' last hope, who was shaking with unbearable sobs as he stood at the plate.

"I protest!" screamed Alex, leaping from the bench and running wildly out to where Nicor stood.

"You have no right to protest," snapped the umpire. "You are merely a spectator."

"Den I pertest!" roared Putzy, skidding to a halt beside Alex. "Turn dat t'ing off!"

At the plate, Casey was melting down in his own tears as the tape swung back into the fifth stanza.

> *Then from the gladdened multitude went up a joyous*
> *   yell.*
> *It rumbled in the mountaintops, it rattled in the dell,*
> *It struck upon the hillside and rebounded on the flat,*
> *For Casey, mighty Casey, was advancing to the bat.*

Casey was flat on the ground now, making feeble pawing motions as if he would dig his grave where he lay, crawl in, and die.

"Your protest is out of order," said Nicor.

Ush Karuza oozed oily sympathy. "I am afraid your batter iss not feeling well," he murmured.

> *. . . And when the writhing pitcher ground his ball into*
> *   his hip,*
> *Defiance gleamed in Casey's eye, a sneer curled*
> *   Casey's lip. . . .*

Abandoning the umpire, Putzy ran to his collapsed star and tried to lift him from the ground. "Fer cripes' sake, Casey," he pleaded. "Stan' up. Just get us one little hit. Dat's all I ask."

"I can't," choked Casey. "Muh heart ain't in it no more. Dey trusted me in Mudville and I let 'em down."

The stillness over the park was broken only by his sobs and the inexorable recorded voice.

> . . . *Close by the sturdy batsman, the ball unheeded*
> *sped.*
> *"That ain't my style," said Casey. "Strike one!" the*
> *umpire said. . . .*

Like a drowning man, Alex saw his whole life parade by him: Tanni, the children, Earth, Toka. It was not what he wanted. He wanted some way out of his inferno.

No other batter had a chance, the Teddies were too demoralized. But what to do, what to do? Surely he, Alexander Jones, had some means of helping, some talent— He gnawed trembling fingers as the poem tolled its way to its dreadful conclusion.

> . . . *And now the air is shattered with the force of*
> *Casey's blow!*

Damn all poets!

> *Oh, somewhere in this favored land the sun is shining*
> *bright,*
> *The band is playing somewhere and somewhere hearts*
> *are light,*
> *And somewhere men are laughing, and somewhere*
> *children shout,*
> *But there is no joy in Mudville—*

Poetry!

–*MIGHTY CASEY HAS STRUCK OUT!*

"Yipe!" said Alex.

There was one other outstanding ability which Ensign Alexander Jones had shown in the Guard besides hitting the dirt. And that was that when the occasion arose, he was very quick off the mark when there was something to be run to, or from. Therefore, just as some weeks earlier the promptitude with which he nosedived would have pleased his superiors, so now they would have joyed to see the speed with which he covered the distance between the umpire's post and the public-address sytem. Even the Professor would have been pushed to match his velocity; and the way he stiff-armed the lone Sarennian guarding the recorder was a privilege to observe.

He snatched up the microphone and panted into it. "Go on, Boss!" yelled Putzy, unsure what his adored plenipotentiary intended but ready to back him up.

"Pant, pant, pant," boomed Alex over the field.

Ush Karuza ran to stop him. "Hold, youth!" ordered Nicor. "He has a right to use the machine."

"Pant, pant," panted Alex, and began to improvise.

> "But hold (pant), what strikes the umpire, what causes
>   him to glare
> With fiery (pant, pant) look and awful eye upon the
>   pitcher there?
> And Casey takes the catcher by the collar with his
>   hand;
> He hales him to the (pant) umpire and together there
>   they stand."

Beside the plate, the Hoka Casey lifted his head in wonder, and wiping the tears from his eyes, stared openmouthed at Alex.

The human had had his dark suspicions about the way Lefty was struck out last time. No chance to prove that, but he could weave it into his revenge.

> " 'I bid you look,' cried Casey, 'I bid you search him
>   well.
> For such as these our fine fair game they soon would
>   sound its knell—' "

Alex hesitated, looking a trifle confused. "Dat's my plenipotentiary who said dat!" cried Putzy's grandmother; and thus heartened, he proceeded.

> "The umpire checks them over and the villains' faces
>   fall
> When out from each one's pocket he pulls forth A
>   HIDDEN BALL!
> 'Oh, shame!' cries out the Mudville crowd. The echoes
>   answer, 'Shame!'
> 'That such a dirty low-down trick should blight our
>   Casey's name.
> The pitcher only faked his throw, the catcher faked his
>   catch.
> The cowards knew that such as they were never Casey's
>   match.' "

"You untentacled mammal!" raged Ush Karuza. "You sslimeless conformation of boned flesh!"

Alex had long ago discovered that mankind rarely reacts to insults couched in nonhuman terms. It did not offend him at all to be told that he was slimeless.

The Teddies' Casey was sitting up by the plate now and beaming. Alex took a deep breath and went on:

> " 'Now take your places once again. Once more!' the
>   umpire cried.
> 'And your next pitches will be fair or else I'll have your
>   hide.
> Now take your places once again, to places one and all!'
> And as soon as they were ready, the umpire cried, 'Play
>   ball.' "

The Hoka Casey was up on his feet and clutching his bat. His eyes were riveted on Alex. And as the last two stanzas came out, his little form hunched and twisted through the motions Alex described.

*"And now the pitcher takes his stance, his face is black
    and grim
And he starts his furious windup with a fearful verve
    and vim.
And now he rocks back on his heel; and now he lets it
    fly.
The ball comes sizzling forward watched by Casey's
    steely eye.*

*"For Casey does not tremble, mighty Casey does not
    balk,
Though it's clear the ball is high and wide, and they
    aim to make him walk.
He steps forward in the batter's box, his bat's a lambent
    flame.
Crack! Smash! The ball flies o'er the fence—AND
    CASEY WINS THE GAME!"*

The stands were going crazy. Hokas of all shapes, sizes, and descriptions came pouring down from their seats to mob and congratulate—

—Casey, of course.

Who else was responsible for the Mudville win?

To Hokan taste, it was almost an anticlimax after the glorious victory of the fictional Casey when the factual one playfully tapped a home run over the left-field fence and won the Sector pennant.

In spite of custom, Alexander Jones did not preside over the wild festivities that night. He felt he deserved a quiet evening at home, alone with a tall drink and *quotation at the waterfront.* Tanni would be coming back soon, and much as he longed to see her, he knew she would give him no chance to produce something really significant—some poem reflecting the realities of Life.

SAREN	2	1	1	1	2	0	6	7	0	20
TOKA	1	0	0	0	0	3	0	15	2	21

MALCOLM JAMESON

A game played with beams of light, selenium
goals, and teams of spacemen leaping and
running in a low-gravity field: that's Dazzle
Dart, the favorite sport of the Space Patrol,
and there's no team better than the one from
the space cruiser *Pollux*. Nor does their
teamwork stop when they leave the court, for
keeping the peace of an entire solar system is
a complicated business. . . .

Malcolm Jameson is little known in science
fiction today, but he was one of the most
popular authors of the 1940's, especially for
his Space Patrol stories. Jameson had been
an officer in the United States Navy, so his
tales of the spacegoing ships of the future always had a ring of authenticity.

Bullard Reflects

"Whee! Yippee! Yow!"

The crowd went crazy. Staid, gold-braided captains and commanders jumped up and down on their seats and yelled themselves hoarse. Even the admirals present dropped their dignified hand clapping for unrestrained shouting. Spacemen of all ratings tossed their hats away, hugged whoever was next to them, and behaved generally like wild men. Alan MacKay had scored his tenth successive goal!

"Castor Beans, Castor Beans—waw! waw! waw!" went the *Pollux* bleachers derisively.

"Polliwogs, Polliwogs—yah, yah, yah!" came the prompt response from the space cruiser *Castor*'s side of the arena. But it was a weak and disheartened chorus. A score of 850 to 25 the wrong way at the end of the first half was not the sort to inspire a cheering section. The *Pollux*'s Dazzle Dart team was mopping up—and how!

Captain Bullard of the *Pollux* was no exception to the rest. He flopped back into his seat red of face and utterly exhausted. His vocal cords had gone long since, and now he could only gasp and speak in weak whispers. Captain Ellington, commander of the mine division, leaned over and congratulated him.

"You've got the General Excellence Trophy in the bag," he said. "That is the third time in a row, isn't it? That means you keep it."

"Yes," said Bullard, feebly. "But, oh, boy, who would have dreamed of picking up a player like this MacKay! I asked for him

45

on account of the way he handled that Jovian surrender, but I had no idea he was such a whiz at Dazzle Dart—"

Then Bullard's husky voice failed him altogether, and he turned to watch the parades between halves.

The interfleet athletic meet, held for the first time since the Jovian armistice, had been a howling success from his point of view from first to last. The hand-picked, well-trained skymen of the *Pollux* had taken every major sport. The meteor-ball contest had been a pushover; they'd earned over eight hundred of the possible thousand points at saltation—that grueling competition of leaping from a stand at all gravities from zero to two and a half. They had outswum, outrun and outplayed their competitors in practically every one of the events. And now, in the most critical test of all, they had a walkaway. He had expected it, of course, but not by such a tremendous margin.

In the meantime the crowd milled and whooped on the plain at the bottom of Luna's well-dome crater Ashtaroth, which was the athletic field of the great Lunar Base. Captain Bullard regained his breath and sat watching. Good boys, his, he was thinking, all of them—whether at war or at play. Then there came another touch at his elbow and Lieutenant Commander Bissel was there, aide to the commandant.

"I hate to inject a serious note into the festivities," he apologized, "but there's something hot coming in over the transether. Remember Egon Ziffler, chief of secret police of the Jovian Empire—the Torturer, they called him?"

Bullard nodded.

"He's been located, and on Titania, of all places. He appeared in a Callistan cruiser and took the place by surprise. Apparently he massacred the entire garrison in the most fiendish manner; the admiral is talking now with the sole survivor who, somehow, managed to escape to Oberon. The worst of it is he is in possession of our experimental arsenal and proving grounds—"

"Yes?" said Bullard.

"Yes. It has not been released yet, but that deadly new electron gun worked perfectly, and there are hundreds of them there. With those in their hands they will be almost invulnerable. Only the screens of a star-class cruiser can resist the hand-size model, and I doubt if those could stand up to the heavier Mark Two we planned to build.''

"That's bad," remarked Bullard, with a sigh. It seemed that no matter how much clean-up work they did, there was always trouble.

"Yes," agreed Bissel, soberly, "it is bad. But I'll toddle along and get the latest. By the time this is over maybe I can give you the full dope.''

He slid out of the box, and Bullard turned his attention once more to the field, only now his thoughts were inside the *Pollux*, parked in her launching rack over at the sky yard. Swiftly he surveyed mentally every compartment in her, then he permitted himself to relax. He could find no fault. She was ready to soar. Just let them give the word.

By that time the playing field was empty. A whistle blew. The second half was about to begin. It seemed a useless waste of time, but the rules were unchangeable. A fleet championship game could not be conceded; it must be played out to the last second.

The Castoreans came onto the field in a somewhat more cheerful frame of mind. In this half they would have the advantage. They had the offensive. Then the Polliwogs tramped in, still jubilant. There was an enormous margin to their credit. They could hardly lose.

The game, essentially, was a simple one. But it called for the utmost a man could develop in alertness, agility and dexterity. Moreover, to get the best results, there must be instant team-work, secured by long practice, for there was scant time to interpret and act upon the sharply barked code signals that demanded various degrees of cooperation.

The elements of it were these. It was played on a court not much different in layout from that required by basketball, football or jai-alai. There were two opposite goals, set high in back-stops. The goals were six-inch black holes in which were selenium units. A semicircular wall, four feet high, guarded a forbidden area at the foot of each backstop. The quarterback of the offensive team had a flashlight—a superflashlight—which was loaded for each half with exactly one hundred ten-second flashes of light. The light was delivered in a thin pencil of one centimeter in diameter, and the inner mechanism of it was so designed that the operator could deliver it one flash at a time by simply pointing it and pressing a button. But once the button was pressed, the light stayed on for a full ten seconds and then went out abruptly, counting as one serve. The idea was to cast the ray into the opposite goal hole. If the bell rang, the quarterback scored twenty-five points.

The defenders' aim was to intercept and deflect the light —into the other goal, if possible. Should they succeed, their score would be double. To effect this, they were equipped with as many slightly convex mirrors as they thought they could handle. The mirrors were not dissimilar from the type worn on the brow of a throat specialist. Players usually wore them strapped to their wrists, but stars could not only manage those, but also ones strapped at their waists and on the hea as well. A good jumper was a distinct asset to a team, and the *Pollux*'s five saltatory champs had been of invaluable assistance.

They took their positions. Weems, captain of the *Castor* team, had the torch. His twenty guards were ranged about him. The Polliwogs scattered out at the other end of the court, tense and waiting. Tackling, holding or slugging was barred, but a man could drop on all fours and make an onrushing opponent stumble over him. There was no more to the game than that.

Weems maneuvered for position, then leaped unexpectedly into the air, and it was a goodly leap, as they were playing on strictly Lunar gravity. At near the top of his flight his hand darted forth and he sent a beam of light at his goal. It struck the backstop not a foot from the goal, but before the eagle-eyed Weems could shift his hand, a Polliwog player was in the air and had caught it with one of his reflectors. A twist of the wrist sent it hurtling back to the other side, a narrow miss. The source of it—Weems—was falling now, and he jerked his arm, throwing the light sharply downward, where one of his own teammates caught it and shot it up at a steep angle under the hovering Polliwog guards. A bull's-eye! And not an instant too soon, for at that moment the light went out. Twenty-five points for the attackers.

So it went—so swiftly the eye could hardly follow. Despite the fact that it was customary to fill the arena dome with humid air and spray dust in it so as to illuminate the darting beam throughout its length, it took the glance of an eagle to keep pace with it. A battery of cameras, of course, recorded the play constantly, and the selenium-cell-operated bell bonged from time to time as the light ray hit it.

The second half was full of brilliant double and triple plays, where often the quarterback would turn and flash his light directly behind him to a confederate, who relayed it across the court, who in his turn shot it into a momentarily undefended goal. The ultimate score, though, was against the Castoreans. Their defeat was so decisive as to admit no quibbling.

The cheering lasted for minutes, but hardly had the final goal bell rung before Bullard was aware that the grand admiral himself had entered his box and was sitting beside him.

"Congratulations," said he, then addressed himself to serious business. "You have already heard a little of what is going on on Titania? I sent Bissel. It is a scurvy trick to recall your crew and send you out on a desperate mission at an hour like this, but there is no other ship ready. Since the armistice it seems that there has been a letdown in discipline. Can you blast off in four hours?"

"I can blast off in one hour if you'll give me an all-Moon hookup on the public-address sytems," said Bullard, without batting an eye. He had not only been expecting the detail, but hoping for it. Ziffler was a creature he loathed from the bottom of his heart—treacherous, cruel and unprincipled, of a breed that extermination is the only cure for.

Within five minutes Bullard was making his appeal to his skymen.

"On the double!" were his last words, and he slammed down the transmitter.

The burned and looted fortress of Caliban lay directly under. Bullard pushed his navigator aside and took the controls himself. He set the antigravs at half strength and slowly lost altitude, constantly searching. At last he found them. There was a parked cruiser of the *Dernfug* class, and a horde of men camped outside alongside it. Phosphorescent flares burned, and he saw they were celebrating. Kegs of the type used as containers for the potent *snahger* liquor rolled all about, and the thickest of the rioting throng were gathered about others yet upright.

"The ship, first," said Bullard grimly, and his gunnery officer—Fraser—said only, "Aye, aye, sir."

The searing, blinding beam of incredible power leaped downward, played a moment on the cruiser, then flickered out. On the ground there was left only a mass of running molted metal, sputtering a valedictory of brilliant sparks.

"Cease firing!" was Bullard's next crisp order. "The grand admiral wants them brought in alive, if possible." He reached for the antigrav control and pushed the deflectors on hard swing.

The *Pollux* came down a mile away to an easy landing on the dark plain. The people in her could plainly see the flood-lamps of the rollicking bandits and the sharp reflections that glinted on the smooth terrain between. There was nothing to impede the progress of the landing force.

But by the time the landing force was ready for its trip, the lookout reported a new development. A party of men was approaching, and they were stretching their arms over their heads in a gesture of surrender. A close scrutiny of them could discover no arms worth worrying about. The new electron projectors were said to be quite heavy, each requiring two men to carry and operate. Any less potent weapon the veterans of the *Pollux* could deal with, and deal with well.

"Find out who they are and what is their proposition," ordered Bullard. "If it sounds reasonable, let three in for a parley. No more. He is full of slimy tricks, that Ziffler. I wouldn't trust his words under any circumstances."

It was not Ziffler, but Skul Drosno, former vice premier of the Jovian regime, together with two high aides. They wanted to arrange terms of surrender, they said. Their story was that they had revolted against the atrocities of Ziffler and had him a prisoner in their camp. They would trade him—trussed up as he was—for personal immunity and a general pardon for their followers. They would willingly submit to trial, knowing now how they had been hoodwinked.

"Let them in," said Bullard, though he was still a trifle doubtful. "I will talk with them."

Skul Drosno began his appeal. Bullard recognized it at once as rank sophistry, but he continued to listen. Then, to his astonishment, Drosno suddenly slumped in his chair. His eyes were crossed to a painful degree, and his hands wavered uncertainly in the air. The next moment he pitched forward onto the deck and sprawled, apparently unconscious. One of his aides looked sick, and staggered to his feet, weaving about ridiculously.

"What an act!" thought Bullard, and sprang to his own feet, alert. He shot a glance to his side and saw that his executive, Moore, who had been with him, was an inert heap. And at that moment things began to blur before his own eyes. His knees wobbled, and he heard a harsh, metallic ringing in his ears. He fought for air, then choked. The floor plates rushed upward and struck him squarely in the face. After that Bullard remembered no more.

The next voice he heard was the high-pitched crackling of the unspeakable Ziffler.

"Can such things be!" crowed the vile Callistan. "A great personage, no less. I find as my prisoner the inimitable, the invincible, the incorruptible Bullard—hero of the nine planets!"

Bullard opened his eyes, ignoring the pounding in the back of his head. He was seated in a chair, strapped hand and foot, and the swaggering ex–police chief who had terrorized the Jovian satellites was standing before him, exulting.

"Perhaps he is not so invincible," pursued his tormentor, calmly lighting a cigarette and seating himself. "We have never seen him outside his formidable *Pollux*. But now that he is in our hands, I am curious to see how good he is. Hagstund! Come here!"

A big brute of a former convict strode forward.

"What do you say? Shall we have a little sport? Why not put

these men in spacesuits and turn them loose for twenty-four
hours? Then we can have a hunt. This man, in particular, has a
gr-r-reat reputation for cleverness. Let's see what he can do on a
barren and resourceless planet. We have counted them, so we
know their numbers. I will give a prize, prizes. Ten thousand
sols for this one, to whoever brings him down. Another ten
thousand for the last man of the lot and another five for the next
to the last. It'll be good fun, eh?"

Ziffler took a swig of *snahger* and delivered himself of an
elaborate wink. Bullard did not believe for a moment he was
drunk. Ziffler was too clever a scoundrel for that. It was a gesture
meant to raise false hopes. Bullard knew all too well what the
wastes of Titania were. He had been there before. Except for the
port of Caliban, the arsenal and a few scattered stations which no
doubt had been plundered by now, there was nothing but bleak,
frozen plains, broken by rugged meteor craters.

"Swell, Chief," agreed the henchman. "What about the
ship?"

"Leave her lie as she is. They'll not send another for days. I
don't want you baboons monkeying around inside her. Let's
give these guys a run, then we'll get down to business. There's
plenty of time."

Rough hands pulled Bullard to his feet, and at the point of
one of the new and deadly electron guns they made him put on
an ordinary spacesuit. As the mists cleared away in his throb-
bing head, he saw that he was in a large hall, and that other men
and officers of his crew were being similarly treated.

"Oh, by the way," remarked Ziffler, offhandedly, "they say I
am unkind. I'll save you one bit of mental torture. What got you
down was our new hypnotic dust. It's very clever, really. Powder
a coat with it, for example, then expose it to air. It vaporizes and
puts everyone to sleep. My emissaries went out, too—naturally.
All but one, that is, who had been heavily doped with an anti-
dote beforehand. He survived long enough to open the door for
us, then, unfortunately, died. It was regrettable, but in my business I find it necessary to do such things."

Bullard said not a word. He was ready. The outlook was
black, but he had seen other outlooks that were quite as black.

"I'll be seeing you, Ziffler," he said, and hoped it was not mere braggadocio. Ziffler had a reputation for sadism, but not for courage. There was the bare chance that that single psychological shot in the dark might in time be digested and unsettle him. "Let's go. I prefer anything to your presence."

"Yeah?" said Ziffler, but he beckoned to his strong-arm squad.

The entire crew of the *Pollux* was there. They were pushed out through the portal of the dome in squads of four and told to get going. Bullard was let out last of all. Their captors promised tauntingly that they had a full Earth day before pursuit.

"Stay together, men," called Bullard into his helmet microphone, the moment the portal closed behind him. "All officers come up close to me."

The light on Titania was dim, even in full daytime. But it was good enough for his officers to read the swift manipulations of his fingers. Their skipper was using the sign language all trained Space Guards men used when they feared their words might be overheard.

"Poleward from here," Bullard told them, "some thirty miles, is a meteorite crater. For several years we have maintained a secret laboratory there and it is possible that these ruffians have not discovered it. That will be our destination. Under this gravity we should reach it within a few hours, though I am uncertain of its exact direction. Have the men spread out and hunt. There should be flares there, and the first man in should light one. The last time I visited the place it had a staff of eight or ten scientists, and an excellent interplanetary radio. They may have weapons, but at least we can flash an alarm."

Rapidly waved arms acknowledged, and the Polliwogs dispersed in the semidarkness.

It was Lieutenant Alan MacKay who reached the spot first. He had trouble in finding a flare, but eventually he found one and lighted it. The laboratory was a shambles. The vandals had found the place, despite his captain's hopes to the contrary, and turned it upside down. The bodies of the physicists and chemists lay all about, and the unhappy director's corpse was discovered nailed to the wall, crucifix style. Torn papers, broken glass and tangled wire littered the floor. The radio had been smashed almost out of recognition. MacKay, a newcomer to the service, shuddered, but he carried out his orders.

Bullard arrived shortly after, and his face was not pretty to see as he viewed the wreckage. Now he regretted the flare. *They* undoubtedly had seen it, too. He had hoped to warn these people, send a message to the System in general, then have his forces scatter. A few of them might have hoped to survive the ruthless man hunt that was to follow.

But the situation was changed, and since any alternative seemed as hopeless as any other, he let the flare continue to burn. By keeping together, some resistance might be improvised. While he was waiting for the stragglers to come up, he busied himself with reassembling the torn pages of the notebooks and journals strewn about the floor.

Much of them dealt with routine analysis, but on a page written in red ink and numbered "97" he found a fragment that brought him to eager attention.

> *Unlike most meteorites, the one that made this crater failed to disintegrate upon impact—or rather, not all of it disintegrated. We have discovered a number of fragments, slightly curved, that indicate it was stratified, and that the stratum of radius, of about thirty meters and of one and a fraction inches in thickness, simply broke into bits instead of molecules. In the storehouse in the crater bottom there are more than a hundred of these fragments, running up as high as twenty centimeters across. They are of a jadelike substance, subject to abrasion by ordinary methods and can be drilled by steel drills, and are not hard and ultradense as might have been expected. The curious thing about these fragments is that they defy X-ray analysis. For some odd reason they wreck every tube that is brought to bear upon them. They backfire, so to speak. Can it be that—*

The page was at an end. Bullard sought frantically for page 98, but he could not find it. He called the trusty Benton.

"Take a gang of men and go down and search the crater. You ought to find a storehouse and in it a bunch of junky-looking rock fragments that look like jade. If you do, bring a flock of them up here. Quick!"

To the others standing around, he said:

"Clear out the wreckage in the workshop and see if those breast drills can be made to work. Strip the boots off those dead men and cut them up into straps. As soon as you have done that, take off your own and cut them up, too. We haven't got time to lose."

Presently Lieutenant Benton came back, and a number of men were with him. They all bore armfuls of slightly curved pieces of a moss-colored, glasslike substance. Each was fairly large, but all had irregular and jagged edges. Bullard examined one hurriedly, hefting it critically.

"Get MacKay up here—quickly," he barked, suddenly. Then he wheeled on Benton. "Take all of these and drill two pairs of holes through each—here and here"—and he showed him. "Then affix straps, just as you would to those mirrors you use in the Dazzle Dart game."

Benton looked at him wonderingly, but he had learned a long time before to put his trust in his remarkable commander. He piled the shiny fragments of meteor stuff together and went out to call in his men.

Bullard felt better. What he was about to attempt was a wild gamble, but it was immeasurably better than waiting like sheep for the slaughter or fleeing hopelessly across the cold wastes of Titania. He was very thankful, too, that on the occasion of his last visit to this satellite he had cut the governor general's party and ball and visited this secluded laboratory instead. For the day he had been here was shortly after the experiments described on the isolated page he now held in his hand. At that time nothing had been definitely determined as to the structure of the mysterious crystalline substance salvaged from the crater, but he recalled the speculations of the now dead scientists concerning it.

Lieutenant MacKay reported.

"Yes, sir?"

"Tell Commander Moore to have all the members of the

Dazzle Dart team report to you here at once, and that means the men on the second team and the scrubs as well. Tell him to have everyone else find pits in the crater bottom and take shelter there until further orders. Clear?"

The ruffians of the Ziffler gang did not play entirely fair, as was to be expected. They beat the gun by several hours. It was Benton, in charge of the lookout, who sighted the mob advancing across the plain. They were in fairly close formation, as if by direction finders or some other means they already knew that the *Pollux* men were not scattered, but together at the so-called Mystery crater.

"Take stations," ordered Bullard, crisply. He was standing in the semidarkness on the crater rim, some distance away from the damaged laboratory. To the right and left of him his victorious Dazzle Dart team were lying behind the irregular parapet made by the crater wall.

"Benton!" he called. "Scatter your squad both ways from me. When that gang of hoodlums is halfway up the hill, let 'em have your flame-gun blast. Then duck and beat it for the bottom of the crater and hide out until I call 'all clear.' "

Benton had found eight old flame guns in a work shed. They had been obsolete as fighting weapons for many years, but could deliver a nasty burn.

Captain Bullard had another look at the advancing hunting party. He saw that they had brought along a number of the new electron guns and were beginning to struggle up to the talus with them. The yelling mob reached a sort of ledge and waited for the guns to be brought up. A jeering voice, louder than the rest, called up:

"Will you come down and take it, you lice, or do we have to come up there and get you?"

"Now!" said Bullard softly into his microphone.

Eight feeble heat machines spat their ruddy blasts, then went out with a jerk as their operators let go of them and slid down the inner wall to safety. It was well that Bullard had foreseen the reply they would get, for the counterblast came almost instantaneously. A score of bright stars flamed out downhill and from them thin streams of almost invisible violet fire lashed upward and played along the crater rim. The rock sprang into incandescence and inches of it melted and flowed as bubbling, sparkling slag down the slope, where it quickly dulled to red and congealed.

"Now?" asked MacKay, anxiously. He was crouched beside the skipper.

"Not yet. Wait until they are closer."

The assault went on for a moment, then stopped. Bullard took a cautious peep and saw the Callistans had resumed their climb.

"What's the dirtiest thing you can call a Callistan?" whispered Bullard, grinning unseen in the dark. "You know the lingo."

"*Froahbortlen*," replied MacKay without hesitation. The Callistan language was rich in epithets, but that one was the most comprehensive and unequivocal ever coined in any language. Even a depraved criminal of the lowest grade would resent it.

"Invite them up," said Bullard, grimly. "When they answer, do your stuff."

"On your toes, men," MacKay warned his teammates. Then he opened his mike wide and issued his sizzling, triple-barreled, insulting invitation.

Bullard involuntarily caught his breath. The die was cast. For an instant one of the qualms of uncertainty that rarely came to him held him in its grip. Was he right, or would they fail? Which side would be the victims of the massacre about to begin? Well, in a couple of seconds he would know.

The properties of the strange meteor substance were still unknown. It stopped gamma and other hard rays. It wrecked the X-ray tubes focused upon it. How could that be, unless it also possessed that long-hunted, but never found, property of being able to deflect and reflect the high-pressure beams?

MacKay's helmet still vibrated with the last vile words of his superb taunt when the answering salve of electric fire came. But that time there was more than inert rock to receive it. A row of alert young men stood on the crest, and a weird-looking crew they were. Glistening bits of rock were strapped to their wrists, to their foreheads, their belts, and even their ankles. In an instant they were leaping, dancing and twisting like mad dervishes, deftly parrying every violet pencil that struck above the rock at their feet. The devastating power was being hurled back whence it came.

The ruffians must have been amazed at the swift return of fire from men they thought to be totally disarmed, but they hung on doggedly for a few seconds more. Then their fire ceased altogether, and all that the observers on the rim could see was a few scared survivors scrambling down the way they had come.

"Too bad we haven't a weapon," sighed Bullard. "We could make a clean sweep."

He whipped out a flashlight and strode down to the ledge. There were many of the abandoned electron guns standing about on tripods, or overturned by the fleeing gangsters. Something soft gave under Bullard's boot. He played his light along the ground and saw a sight that under other circumstances would have been revolting. Loose hands and feet, attached to charred stumps of arms or legs, were strewn widely. Other and less readily identifiable fragments of disintegrated humanity lay among them. Ziffler's strong-arm squad, once the terror of the outer planets, had been dispersed in the fullest sense of the word.

Bullard turned on his amplifier.

"Okay, Moore. Round up the men and bring them down. We're going back."

The trek back across the icy waste seemed infinitely shorter and easier than it had on the outward journey. Men's hearts were light now, and not leaden as before. To the Polliwogs, the knowledge they had lost their ship had been as dispiriting as the seeming certainty of their impending doom. Now all that was changed. A mile ahead of them lay the *Pollux*, just as they had left her.

The search for Ziffler and the stragglers took some time, but they found them, cowering and whimpering behind a boulder.

"Iron them well and throw them into the brig," snapped Bullard, and went into his ship.

He grabbed a signal pad and wrote a brief report.

A little later the grand admiral at Lunar Base stretched out his hand for the flimsy bit of yellow paper his orderly had brought him. He read it, then read it again. He frowned a little and scratched his head.

"Has Bullard gone highbrow on us, or what the hell?" he asked, tossing the message over to Bissel. Bissel picked it up and read:

After reflection, the enemy succumbed.

                                                                Bullard

KEITH LAUMER

Ever wish you were taller, so you could see over people in a crowd? Or small and fast, for outmaneuvering others? Or maybe you'd like better eyesight, or to be more handsome or beautiful. . . . Well, if you lived in the future world Keith Laumer imagines here, you could have a closetful of bodies for all occasions — including fights in the gladiatorial arena, where you might be facing someone wearing a Charlemagne body but you wouldn't be overmatched if you had an Atlas yourself. It makes for a very different sort of contest.

Keith Laumer is justly famed as a writer of science-fiction adventure stories with a twist of humor. He's rarely been in better form than in *The Body Builders*.

The Body
Builders

I

He was a big bruiser in a Gendye Mark Seven Sullivan, the luxury model with the nine-point sensory system, the highest-priced Grin-U-Matic facial expression attachment on the market and genuine human hair, moustache and all.

He came through the dining-room entry like Genghis Khan invading a Swiss convent. If there'd been a door in his way he'd have kicked it down. The two lads walking behind him—an old but tough-looking utility model Liston and a fairly new Wayne—kept their hands in their pockets and flicked their eyes over the room like buggy whips. The head waiter popped out with a stock of big purple menus, but the Sullivan went right past him, headed across toward my table like a field marshal leading a victory parade.

Lorena was with me that night, looking classy in a flossed-up Dietrich that must have set her back a month's salary. She was in her usual mood for the usual reason: she wanted to give up her job at the Cent-Prog and sign a five-year marriage contract with me. The idea left me cold as an Eskimo's tombstone. In the first place, at the rate she burned creds, I'd have to creak around in a secondhand Lionel with about thirty percent sensory coverage and an undersized power core; and in the second, I was still carrying the torch for Julie. Sure, Julie had nutty ideas about Servos. According to her, having a nice wardrobe of specialized outfirts for all occasions was one step below cannibalism.

63

"You and that closetful of zombies!" She used to shake her finger under my nose. "How could a girl possibly marry you and never know what face she'd see when she woke up in the morning!"

She was exaggerating, but that was the way those Organo-Republicans are. No logic in 'em. After all, doesn't it make sense to keep your organic body on file in the Municipal Vaults, safe out of the weather, and let a comfortable, late-model Servo do your walking and talking? Our grandparents found out it was a lot safer and easier to sit in front of the TV screen with feely and smelly attachments than to be out bumping heads with a crowd. It wasn't long after that that they developed the contact screens to fit your eyeballs, and the plug-in audio, so you began to get the real feel of audience participation. Then, with the big improvements in miniaturization and the new tight-channel transmitters, you could have your own private man-on-the-street pickup. It could roam, seeing the sights, while you sacked out on the sofa.

Of course, with folks spending so much time flat on their backs, the Public Health boys had to come up with gear to keep the organic body in shape. For a while, people made it with part-time exercise and home-model massage and feeding racks, but it wasn't long before they set up the Central File system.

Heck, the government already had everything about you on file, from your birth certificate to your fingerprints. Why not go the whole hog and file the body too?

Of course, nobody had expected what would happen when the quality of the sensory pickups and playbacks got as good as they did. I mean the bit the eggheads call "personality gestalt transfer." But it figured. A guy always had the feeling that his consciousness was sitting somewhere back of his eyes; so when the lids were linked by direct hookup to the Servo, and all the other senses tied in—all of a sudden, you were *there*. The brain was back in Files, doped to the hairline, but you—the thing you call a mind—was there, inside the Servo, living it up.

And with that kind of identification, the old-type utilitarian models went out of style, fast. People wanted Servos that expressed the real inner man—the guy you should have been. With everybody as big and tough as they wanted to be, depending on the down payment they could handle, nobody wanted to take any guff off anybody. In the old days, a fellow had to settle for a little fender-bending; now you could hang one on the other guy, direct. Law Cent had to set up a code to cover the problem, and now when some bird insulted you or crowded you off the Fastwalk, you slugged it out with a Monitor watching.

Julie claimed it was all a bunch of nonsense; that the two Servos pounding each other didn't prove anything. She could never see that with perfect linkage, you *were* the Servo. Like now: The waiter had just put a plate of *consommé au beurre blanc* in front of me, and with my high-priced Yum-gum palate accessory, I'd get the same high-class taste thrills as if the soup were being shoved down my Org's mouth in person. It was a special mixture, naturally, that lubricated my main swivel and supplied some chemicals to my glandular analogs. But the flavor was there.

And meanwhile, the old body was doing swell on nutrient-drip into the femoral artery. So it's a little artificial maybe—but what about the Orggies, riding around in custom-built cars that are nothing but substitute personalities, wearing padded shoulders, contact lenses, hearing aids, false teeth, cosmetics, elevator shoes, rugs to cover their bald domes? If you're going to wear false eyelashes, why not false eyes? Instead of a nose bob, why not bob the whole face? At least a fellow wearing a Servo is honest about it, which is more than you can say for an Orggie doll in a foam-rubber bra—not that Julie needed any help in that department.

I dipped my big silver spoon in and had the first sip just under my nose when the Sullivan slammed my arm with his hip going past. I got the soup square in the right eye. While I was still clicking the eyelid, trying to clear the lens, the Liston jarred my shoulder hard enough to rattle my master solenoid.

Normally, I'm a pretty even-tempered guy. It's my theory that the way to keep a neurotronic system in shape is to hold the glandular inputs to a minimum. But, what with the big event coming up that night, and Lorena riding me hard on the joys of contract life, I'd had a hard day. I hopped up, overrode the eye-blink reflex, made a long reach and hooked a finger in the Liston collar going away.

"Hold it right there, stumblebum!" I gave the collar a flick to spin him around.

He didn't spin. Instead, my elbow joint made a noise like a roller skate hitting loose gravel; the jerk almost flipped me right on my face.

The Liston did a slow turn, like a ten-ton crane rig, looked me over with a pair of yellow eyes that were as friendly as gun barrels. A low rumbling sound came out of him. I was a little shook but mad enough not to let it bother me.

"Let's have that license number," I barked at him. "There'll be a bill for the eye and another one for a chassis checkup!"

The Wayne had turned, too, and was beetling his brows at me. The big-shot Sullivan pushed between the two of them, looked me over like I was something he'd found curled up in a doorway.

"Maybe you better kind of do a fade, Jasper," he boomed loud enough for everybody in the restaurant to hear. "My boy's got no sense of humor."

I had my mouth open for my next mistake when Lorena beat me to it:

"Tell the big boob to get lost, Barney; he's interrupting what I was saying to you."

The Sullivan rolled an eye at her, showing off his independent suspension. "Shut your yap, sister," he said.

That did it. I slid my left foot forward, led with a straight left to the power pack, then uppercut him with everything I was able to muster.

My right arm went dead to the shoulder. The Sullivan was still standing there, looking at me. I was staring down at my own fist, dangling at my side. Then it dawned on me what was wrong.

For the moment, I'd forgotten I was wearing a light sport-model body.

2

Gully Fishbein, my business manager, Servo-therapist, drinking buddy, arena trainer and substitute old-maid aunt had warned me I might pull a stunt like this some day. He was a single—Servo Socialist himself, and in addition to his political convictions, he'd put a lot of time and effort into building me up as the fastest man with a net and mace in show business. He had an investment to protect.

"I'm warning you, Barney," he used to shove an untrimmed hangnail under my nose and yell. "One day you're gonna get your reflexes crossed and miss your step on the Fastwalk—or gauge a close one like you was wearing your Astaire and bust the neck of that Carnera you wasted all that jack on. And then where'll you be, hah?"

"So I lose a hulk," I'd come back. "So what? I've got a closetful of spares."

"Yeah? And what if it's a total? You ever heard what can happen to your mind when the connection's busted—and I do mean busted—like that?"

"I wake up back in my Org body; so what?"

"Maybe." Gully would shake his head and look like a guy with dangerous secrets. "And maybe not . . ."

While I was thinking all this, the Sullivan was getting his money's worth out of the Grin-U-Matic. He nodded and rocked back on his heels, taking his time with me. The talk had died out at the tables around us. Everybody was catching an earful.

"A wisy," the Sullivan said, loud. "What's the matter, Cheapie, tired of life outside a repair depot?"

"What do you mean, 'Cheapie'?" I said, just to give my Adam's apple a workout. "This Arcaro cost me plenty . . . and this goon of yours has jarred my contacts out of line. Just spring for a checkup and I'll agree to forget the whole thing."

"Yeah." He was still showing me the expensive grin. "I'll bet you will, pint-size." He cocked an eye at the Wayne. "Now, let's see, Nixie. Under the traffic code, I got a couple courses of action, right?"

"Cream duh pansy and let's shake a ankle, Boss. I'm hungry." Nixie folded a fist like a forty-pound stake mallet and moved in to demonstrate his idea.

"Nah." The Sullivan stopped him with the back of his hand against his starched shirt front. "The guy pops me first, right? He wants action. So I give him action. Booney." He snapped his fingers and the Liston thumbed a shirt stud.

"For the record," the Sullivan said in a businesslike voice. "Notice of Demand for Satisfaction, with provocation, under Section Nine-Ninety-One-b, Granyauck Six-Seventy-Eight." I heard the whir and click as the recorder built into the Liston's thorax took it down and transmitted it to Law Central.

All of a sudden my mouth was dry.

Sometimes those Servo designers got a little too realistic. I tapped a switch in my lower-right premolar to cut out the panic-reaction circuit. I'd been all set for a clip on the jaw, an event that wouldn't be too good for the Arcaro, but nothing a little claim to Law Cent wouldn't fix up. But now it was dawning like sunrise over Mandalay that Big Boy had eased me into a spot—or that I'd jumped into it, mouth first; *I'd hit him*. And the fact that he'd put my consommé in my eye first wouldn't count—not to Law Cent. He had the right to call me out—a full-scale Servo-to-Servo match—and the choice of weapons, ground, time, everything was his.

"Tell the manager to clear floor number three," the Sullivan rapped out to the Wayne. "My favorite ground." He winked at Lorena. "Nine kills there, baby. My lucky spot."

"Whatever you say." I felt myself talking too fast. "I'll be back here in an hour, raring to go."

"Nix, Cheapie. The time is now. Come as you are; I ain't formal."

"Why, you can't do that," Lorena announced. Her voice tapes were off key, I noticed; she had a kind of shill, whiny tone. "Barney's only wearing that little old Arcaro!"

"See me after, doll," the Sullivan cut her off. "I like your style." He jerked his head at the Wayne. "I'll take this clown bare-knuck, Mixie, Naples rules." He turned away, flexing the oversized arms that were an optional extra with the late-model Gendyes. Lorena popped to her feet, gave me the dirtiest look the Dietrich could handle.

"You and that crummy Arcaro." She stuck it in me like a knife. "I wanted you to get a Flynn, with the—"

"Spare me the technical specs, kid," I growled. I was getting the full picture of what I'd been suckered into. The caper with the soup hadn't been any accident. The timing was perfect; I had an idea the Liston was wired a lot better than he looked. Somebody with heavy credits riding on that night's bout was behind it; somebody with enough at stake to buy all the muscle-Servos he needed to pound me into a set of loose nerve ends waving around like worms in a bait can. Busting the Arcaro into a pile of scrap metal and plastic wouldn't hurt my Org physically—but the trauma to my personality, riding the Servo, would be for real. It took steel nerve, cast-iron confidence, razor-edge reflexes and a solid killer's instinct to survive in the arena. After all, anybody could lay out for a Gargantua Servo, if that was all it took; the timing, and pace, and ringcraft that made me a winner couldn't survive having a body pounded to rubble around me. I'd be lucky if I ever recovered enough to hold a coffee cup one-handed.

The Floor Manager arrived, looking indignant; nobody had called him to okay the fracas. He looked at me, started to wave me off, then did a double-take.

"*This* is the aggressor party?" the eyebrows on his Menjou crawled up into his hairline.

"That's right." I gave it to him fast and snappy. "The bum insulted my lady friend. Besides which, I don't like his soup strainer. After I break his rib cage down to chopsticks, I'm going to cut half of it off and give it to the pup to play with." After all, if I was going to get pulverized, I might as well do it in style.

The Sullivan growled.

"You can talk better than that." I pushed up close to him; my nose was on a level with the diamond stickpin in his paisley foulard. "What's your name, Big Stuff? Let's have that registration."

"None of your pidgin, Wisy." He had a finger all ready to poke at me, saw the Monitor coming up ready to quote rules, used it to scratch his ear instead. The big square fingernail shredded plastic off the lobe; he was a little more nervous than he acted. That cinched it: he knew who I was—Barney Ramm, light-heavy champ in the armed singles.

"Assembly and serial numbers, please," the Monitor said. He sounded a little impatient. I could see why he might. It was customary for a challenger to give him the plate data without being asked—especially a floor vet like Sullivan. He was giving the official a dirty look.

"Where's Slicky?" he growled.

"He doesn't come on for another fifteen minutes," the Monitor snapped. "Look here—"

"*You* look here, Short-timer," the Sullivan grunted. The Wayne moved up to help him give the fellow the cold eye. He glared back at them—for about two seconds. Then he wilted. The message had gotten through. The fix was in.

"Where's the men's room?" I piped up, trying to sound as frisky as ever, but at the moment my mind felt as easy to read as a ninety-foot glare sign.

"Eh?" The Monitor cut his eyes at me, back at the Sullivan, back to me, like a badminton fan at a championship match. "No," he said. He pushed out his lips and shook his head. "I'm ruling—"

"Rule my foot." I jostled him going past. "I know my rights." I kept going, marched across the dance floor to the discreet door back of the phony palm tree. Inside, I went into high gear. There was a row of coin-operated buffing and circuit-checking machines down one wall, a power-core dispenser, a plug-in recharge unit, a nice rack of touch-up paints, a big bin of burned-out reflex coils, and a dispenser full of replacement gaskets with a sign reading: FOR SAFETY'S SAKE—PREVENTS HOT BEARINGS.

I skidded past them, dived through an archway into the service area. There were half a dozen padded racks here, loops of power leads, festoons of lube conduit leading down from ceiling-mounted manifolds. A parts index covered the far wall. There was no back door.

"Kindly take (*click*) position numbered one," a canned voice cackled at me. "Use the console provided to indicate required services. Say, fellow, may I recommend this week's special, Slideeze, the underarm lubricant with a diff——"

I slapped the control plate to shut the pitch off. Coming in here suddenly didn't seem as cute as it had ten seconds earlier. I was cornered—and an accident on a lube-rack would save any possible slip-up on the floor. A little voice about as subtle as a jackhammer was yelling in my ear that I had half a minute, if I was lucky, before a pair of heavies came through the door to check me out. . . .

It was three quick steps to the little stub wall that protected the customers from the public eye. I flattened myself against the wall beside it just as big feet clumped outside. The door banged open. The Wayne wasn't bothering about being subtle. I wasn't either. I hooked his left instep, spun in behind him, palmed his back hard. He hit face first with a slam like two garbage flats colliding, and started looping the loop on the tiled floor. Those Waynes always did have a glass jaw. I didn't stick around to see if anybody heard him pile in; I jumped over him, slid out through the door. The Liston was standing on the other side of the palm, not ten feet away. I faded to the right, saw another door. The glare sign above it said LADIES. I thought it over for about as long as it takes a clock to say *tick* and dived through.

3

Even under the circumstances it was kind of a shock to find myself standing there staring at pink and turquoise service racks, gold-plated perfume dispensers, and a big display rack full of strictly feminine spares that were enough to make a horse blush.

Then I saw *her*. She was a neat-looking Pickford—the traditional models were big just then. She had fluffy blond hair, and her chassis covers were off to the waist. I gaped at her, sitting there in front of the mirror, then gulped like a seal swallowing a five-pound salmon. She jumped and swiveled my way, and I got a load of big blue eyes and a rosebud mouth that was opening up to scream.

"Don't yell, lady!" I averted my eyes—an effort like uprooting saplings. "The mob's after me. Just tell me how to get out of here!"

I heard feet outside. So did she, I guess.

"You—you can go out through the delivery door," a nice

little voice said. I flicked an eye her way. She was holding a lacy little something over her chest. It slipped when she pointed and I got an eyeful of some of the nicest molded foam-plastic you'd care to see.

"Thanks, baby, you're a doll," I choked out and went past her, not without a few regrets. The door she'd shown me was around a corner at the back. There was a big cartonful of refills for the cosmetics vendor beside it, with the top open. On impulse, I reached in and grabbed one going past.

The door opened into an alley about four feet wide, with a single-rail robo-track down the center for service and delivery mechs. The wall opposite was plain duralith; it went up, a sheer rise without a foothold for a gnat. In both directions the alley was a straight shot for fifty feet to a rectangle of hard late-afternoon sunlight. I could take my choice.

Something clattered to the right. I saw a small custodial cart move jerkily out of a doorway, swing my way, picking up speed. I started to back away; the thing was heavy enough to flatten my Arcaro without slowing down. Then a red light blinked on the front of the thing. It made screechy noises and skidded to a stop.

"Kindly clear the rail," a fruity voice hooted. "This is your busy Sani-mat Service Unit, bringing that Sani-mat sparkle to another satisfied customer!"

A kind of idea formed up somewhere under my hairpiece. I eased around to the side of the machine, a tight squeeze. It was a squatty, boxy job, with a bunch of cleaning attachments racked in front and a good-sized bin behind, half full of what it had been collecting. I got the lid up, climbed up as it started forward again, and settled down in the cargo. I was lumpy and wet, and you could have hammered the aroma out into horsehoes. I guess the world has made a lot of progress in the last few decades, but garbage still smells like garbage.

I estimated I'd covered a hundred feet or less, when the cart braked to a sudden stop. I heard voices; something clicked and a hum started up near my left ear.

"Kindly clear the rail," the tape said. "This is your Sani-mat Service Uuwwrrr—"

The cart jumped and I got another faceful of garbage.

Somebody—it sounded like the Wayne—yelled something. I got set, ready to come out swinging as I heard running feet. The cart started up, bumped along clucking to itself like a chicken looking for a place to drop an egg. I rode it along to its next client's back door, then hopped out, legged it to a public screen booth and dialed Gully's number.

4

I caught him in a cab, just dropping in past a mixed-up view of city skyline tilting by in the background. His eyes bugged out like a Chihuahua's when I told him—a de luxe feature of the four-year-old Cantor he always wore.

"Barney, you nuts?" He had a yelp like a Chihuahua too. "The biggest bout of your career coming up tonight, and you're mixing in a free brawl!" He stopped to gulp and ran his eyes over me. "Hey, Barney! You're wearing an Arcaro. You didn't—"

"The fracas wasn't my idea," I got in quick while he was fighting the Cantor's tonsils back in line. "Not exactly, anyway. I took off out the back way, and—"

"You did *what*?" The yelp was up into the supersonic now.

"I beat it. Ducked out. Scrammed. What do you think I was going to do, stay there and let that elbow squad pull the legs off me like a fly?"

"You can't run out on a registered satisfaction, Barney!" Gully leaned into his sender until all I could see were two eyes like bloodshot clams and a pair of quivering nostrils. "You, of all people! If the Pictonews Services get hold of this, they'll murder you!"

"This hit squad will murder me quicker—and not just on paper!"

"Paper's what I'm talking about! You're the aggressor party; you poked the schlock! You cop a swiftie on this, and you're a fugitive from Law Cent! They'll lift your Servo license, and it'll be good-by, career! And the fines—"

"Okay—but I got a few rights too! If I can get to another Servo before they grab me, it'll become my legal *corpus operandi* as soon as I'm in it. Remember, that satisfaction is to me, Barney Ramm, not to this body I'm wearing. You've got to get me out of here, and back to my apartment—" I felt my mouth freeze in the open position. Fifty feet away, across the Fastwalk, the Liston and a new heavy, a big, patched-up Baer, had come out of a doorway and were standing there, looking over the crowd. Those boys were as hard to shake loose as gum on a shoe sole. I ducked down in the booth.

"Listen, Gully," I hissed. "They're too close; I've got to do a fast fade. Try to fix it with Law Cent to keep their mitts off me until I can change. Remember, if they catch me, you can kiss your ten percent good-bye."

"Barney, where you going? Whattaya mean, ten percent? It ain't the cookies I'm thinking about!"

"Think about the cookies, Gully." I cut contact and risked a peek. The two goons were still there and looking my way. If I stepped out, they'd have me. And if I stayed where I was, sooner or later they'd get around to checking the booth. . . .

I was still holding something in my hand. I looked at it: the cosmetics kit I'd grabbed on the way out of the ladies' room at the Troc.

The lid flipped back when I touched the little gold button at the side. There were nine shades of eye shadow, mouth paint, plastic lens shades in gold, green and pink—some dames have got screwy ideas about what looks attractive—spare eyebrows and lashes, a little emergency face putty, some thimble-sized hair sprays.

I hated to ruin a hundred-cee wig, but I gave it a full shot of something called Silver Ghost. The pink eyes seemed to go with the hair. The spray was all gone, and it was too late to bleach a set of eyebrows, so I used a pair of high-arched black ones, then used a gingery set for a moustache. I thought about using one of the fake spit curls for a goatee, but decided against it. The Arcaro had a nice-sized nose on it, so I widened the nostrils a little and added warts. I risked another peek. The boys were right where I left them.

My jacket was a nice chartreuse job with cerise stripes and a solid orange lining. I turned it inside out, ditched the yellow tie, and opened my shirt collar so the violet part showed. That was about all I could do; I opened the door and stepped out.

I'd gone about three steps when the Carnera looked my way. His mouth dropped open like a power shovel getting ready to take a big bite out of a hillside. He jammed an elbow into the Liston and he turned around and *his* mouth fell open. I got a glimpse of some nice white choppers and a tongue like a pink sock. I didn't wait to catch the rest of the reaction: I sprinted for the nearest shelter, a pair of swinging doors, just opening to let a fat Orggie out.

I dived past him into a cool, dark room lit by a couple of glowing beer ads above a long mirror with a row of bottles. I charged past all that, slammed through a door at the back, and was out in an alley, looking at the Wayne. He went into a half-crouch and spread his arms. That was the kind of mistake an amateur toughie would make. I put my head down and hit him square under his vest button. It wasn't the best treatment in the world for the Arcaro, but it was worse for the Wayne. He froze up and made a noise like frying fat, with his eyeballs spinning like Las Vegas cherries. Between the fall in the john and the butt in the neuro center, he was through for the day.

I got my legs under me and started off at a sort of cripple's lope toward the end of the alley.

My balance and coordination units were clicking like castanets. I ricocheted off a couple of walls, made it out into the Slowwalk, and jigged along in a crabbed semicircle, making jerky motions with my good arm at a cab that picked then to drop a fare a few yards away. The hackie reached out, grabbed my shoulder and hauled me inside. Those boys may be built into their seats and end at the waist, but they've got an arm on them. I'll give 'em that.

"You look like you got a problem there, Mac." He looked me over in the mirror. "What happened, you fall off a roof?"

"Something like that. Just take me to the Banshire Building, fast."

"Whatever you say, bud. But if I was you, I'd get that Servo to a shop as quick as I could."

"Later. Step on it."

"I'm doing a max and a half now!"

"Okay, okay, just don't waste any time." He muttered to

himself then, while I got the bent cover off my rest panel and did what I could to rebalance my circuitry. My double vision cleared a little, and the leg coordination improved enough so I managed to climb out unassisted when he slammed the heli in hard on the roof deck.

"Be five cees," the cabbie grunted. I paid him. "Stick around a few minutes," I said. "I'll be right back."

"Do me a favor, Clyde; throw your trade to the competition." He flipped the flag up and lifted off in a cyclone of overrevved rotors. I spat out a mouthful of grit and went in through the fancy door with the big gold B.

Gus, the doorman, came out of his cage with his admiral's hat on crooked; he hooked a thumb over his shoulder and got his jaw all set for the snappy line. I beat him to it.

"It's me, Barney Ramm. I'm incommunicado to avoid the fans."

"Geeze, Mr. Ramm? Wow, that Arcaro won't never be the same again. Looks like your fans must of caught you after all." He showed me a bunch of teeth that would have looked at home in a mule's face. I lifted a lip at him and went on in.

5

My apartment wasn't the plushest one in the Banshire, but it was fully equipped. The Servo stall was the equal of anything at Municipal Files. I got enough cooperation out of my legs to hobble to it, got the Arcaro into the rack with the neck plate open and the contacts tight against the transfer disk.

A pull on the locking lever, and I was clamped in tight, ready for the shift. I picked the Crockett; it was rugged enough to handle the Sullivan, and didn't have any fancy equipment installed to have to look out for. It was a little tough coding the number into the panel, but I made it, then slammed the transfer switch.

I've never gotten used to that wild couple of seconds while the high-speed scanner is stripping the stored data off one control matrix and printing it on another one linking it in to the Org brain back between my real ears in the cold files downtown. It was like diving into an ocean of ice-cold darkness, spinning like a Roman candle. All kinds of data bits flash through the conscious level: I was the Arcaro, sitting rigid in the chair, and I was also the Crockett, clamped to a rack in the closet, and at the same time I could feel the skull contacts and servicing tubes and the cold slab under me in the Vault. Then it cleared and I was hitting the release lever and stepping out of the closet and beginning to feel like a million bucks.

The Arcaro looked pretty bad, sagging in the stall, with the phony eyebrows out of line and the putty nose squashed, and the right shoulder humped up like Quasimodo. It was a wonder it had gotten me back at all. I made myself a promise to give it the best overhaul job money could buy—that was the least I could do. Then I headed for the front door.

The Sullivan would get a little surprise when I found him now. I gave my coonskin cap a pat as I went by the hall mirror, palmed the flush panel open and ran smack into four large cops, standing there waiting for me.

It was a plush jailhouse, as jails go, but I still didn't like it. They shoved me into a nice corner cell with a carpet, a tiled lube cubicle in the corner, and a window with a swell view of Granyauck—about eighteen hundred feet straight down. There were no bars, but the wall was smooth enough to discourage any human flies from trying it.

The turnkey looked me over and shook his head. He was wearing the regulation Police Special, a dumb-looking production job halfway between a Kildare and a Tracy—Spence, that is. I guess cops have to have a uniform, but the sight of a couple dozen identical twins standing around kind of gives a fellow a funny feeling—like Servos were just some kind of robot, or something.

"So you're Barney Ramm, huh?" The cop shifted his toothpick to the other corner of his mouth. "You shunt of tried to handle four cops at once, buddy. Your collision insurance don't cover that kind of damage."

"I want my manager!" I yelled as loud as I could, which wasn't very loud on account of a kick in the voice box I got following up too close on a cop I had tossed on his ear. "You can't do this to me! I'll get the lot of you for false arrest!"

"Relax, Ramm." The jailer waved his power-billie at me to remind me he had it. I shied off; a shot from the hot end of that would lock my neuro center in a hard knot. "You ain't going noplace for a while," the cop stated. "Commissioner Malone wouldn't like it."

"Malone? The arena commissioner? What's he got—" I stopped in the middle of the yell, feeling my silly look freeze in place.

"Yeah," the cop said. "Also the police commissioner. Seems like Malone don't like you, Ramm."

"Hey!" A dirty idea was growing. "The satisfaction against me: who filed it?"

The cop went through the motions of yawning. "Lessee . . . oh, yeah. A Mr. Malone."

"The dirty crook! That's illegal! I was framed!"

"You slugged him first, right?" The cop cut me off.

"Sure, but—"

"Ain't a police commissioner got as much right as anybody else to defend hisself? Any reason he's got to take guff off some wisenheimer, any more than the next guy? You race him at the light, he'll lock bumpers with you every time!"

"I've got to get out of here!" I shouted him down. "Get Gully Fishbein! He'll post the bond! I've got a bout at the Garden in less than four hours! Tell the judge! I guess I've got a couple rights!"

"You ain't going to make no bout in no four hours." The cop grinned like Sears foreclosing on Roebuck. "You'll be lucky if you get out before Christmas holidays start, in September."

"If I don't," I said, "you can start scanning the Help-Wanted—Cripple column. That's what you'll be when me and my twenty-thousand-cee Charlemagne finish with you, you dumb flatfoot!"

He narrowed his eyes down to pinpoints—an extra-cost feature that the taxpayers had to spring for. "Threats, hah?" His voice had the old gravel in it now. "You run out on a satisfaction, buster. That's trouble enough for most guys."

"I'll show you trouble," I started, but he wasn't through yet.

"For a big tough arena fighter, you got kind of a delicate

stomach, I guess. We also got you for resisting arrest, damaging public property, committing mayhem on the person of a couple honest citizens, Peeping Tom, and shoplifting from the ladies' john. You're set for tonight, pal—and a lotta other nights." He gave me a mock salute and backed out; the glass door clinked in my face while I was still trying to get my arm back for a swing.

The watch set in my left wrist was smashed flat, along with the knuckles. Those Granyauck cops have got hard heads. I went over to the window and checked the sun.

It looked like about half past four. At 8 P.M. the main event would go on. If I wasn't there, the challenger would take the title by default. He was an out-of-town phony known as Mysterious Marvin, the Hooded Holocaust; he always fought with a flour sack over his face. After tonight, he'd be light-heavy champ, bagged head and all—and I'd be a busted has-been, with my accounts frozen, my contract torn up, my Servo ticket lifted, and about as much future as a fifth of bourbon at a baptist Retreat. It was the finish. They had me. Unless . . .

I poked my head out and looked down the wall. It was a sheer drop to a concrete loading apron that looked about the size of a blowout patch from where I stood. I felt my autonomics kick in; my heart started thumping like an out-of-round drive shaft, and my throat closed up like a crapshooter's fist. I never had liked heights much. But with my Servo locked in a cell—and me locked in the Servo . . .

I took a couple turns up and down the cell. It was an idea the boys talked about sometimes, waiting in the service racks before a bout: What would happen if the plastic-foam and wire-sponge information correlation unit where the whole brain pattern was recorded got smashed flat—wiped out—while you were in it?

It would be like dreaming you fell—and hit. Would you ever wake up? The Org body was safe, back in the Vaults, but the shock—what would it do to you?

There were a lot of theories. Some of the guys said it would be curtains. The end. Some of them said your Org would go catatonic. I didn't know, myself. If the wheels knew, they weren't spreading it around.

And there was just the one way to find out for sure.

If I stayed where I was, incommunicado, I was finished anyway. Better to go out in style. Before I could change my mind, I whirled, went to the window and swung my legs over the sill. Behind me, I heard somebody yell, "Hey!" I tried to swallow, couldn't, squeezed my eyes shut and jumped. For a few seconds, it was like a tornado blowing straight up into my face; then it was like being spread-eagled on a big, soft, rubbery mattress. And then—

6

I was drowning in a sea of rancid fat. I took a deep breath to yell, and the grease in my lungs clogged solid.

I tried to cough and couldn't do that either. Little red skyrockets started shooting around back of my eyes like fire in a fireworks factory. Then the lights ran together and I was staring at a long red glare strip set in a dark ceiling a few inches above my face. I could feel tubes and wires dragging at my arms and legs, my neck, my eyelids, my tongue. . . .

I was moving, sliding out into brighter light. A scared-looking face was gaping down at me. I made gargly noises and flapped my hands—about all I could manage under the load of spaghetti. The guy leaning over me jumped like a morgue attendant seeing one of his customers sit up and ask for a light, which wasn't too far off, maybe. My bet had paid off. I was awake, back in my organic body in slot number 999/1-Ga8b in the Municipal Body Files.

The next half hour was a little hectic. First they started some kind of a pump, and then I could breathe—a little. While I coughed, twitched, groaned, itched, throbbed and ached in more places than I knew I had, the file techs fussed over me like midwives delivering a TV baby. They pulled things out, stuck things in, sprayed me, jabbed me, tapped and tested, conferred, complained, ran back and forth, shone lights in my eyes, hit me with little hammers, poked things down my throat, held buzzers to my ears, asked questions and bitched at each other in high, whining voices like bluebottle flies around a honey wagon. I got the general idea. They were unhappy that I had upset the routine by coming out of a stage-three storage state unannounced.

"There are laws against this sort of thing!" a dancy little bird in an unhealthy-looking Org body kept yelling at me. "You might have died! It was sheer good fortune that I happened to have slipped back in the stacks to commune with myself, and heard you choking! You frightened me out of my wits!"

Somebody else shoved a clipboard in front of me. "Sign this," he said. "It's a release covering Cent Files against any malpractice or damage claims."

"And there'll be an extra service charge on your file for emergency reprocessing," the dancy one said. "You'll have to sign that, and also an authorization to transfer you to dead storage until your next of kin or authorized agent brings in the Servo data—"

I managed to sit up. "Skip the reprocessing," I said. "And the dead storage. Just get me on my feet and show me the door."

"How's that? You're going to need at least a week's rest, a month's retraining, and a complete reorientation course before you can be released in Org——"

"Get me some clothes," I said. "Then I'll sign the papers."

"This is blackmail!" Dancy did a couple of steps. "I won't be held responsible!"

"Not if you cooperate. Call me a cab." I tried walking. I was shaky, but all things considered I didn't feel too bad—for a guy who'd just committed suicide. Files had kept me in good condition.

There was a little more argument, but I won. Dancy followed me out, wagging his head and complaining, but I signed his papers and he disappeared—probably to finish communing with himself.

In the cab, I tried to reach Gully again. His line was busy. I tried Lorena. A canned voice told me her line was disconnected. Swell. All my old associates were kind of fading out of sight, now that I was having trouble with the law.

But maybe Gully was just busy getting me a postponement. In fact, he was probably over at the Garden now, straightening things out. I gave the hackie directions and he dropped me by the big stone arch with the deep-cut letters that said FIGHTERS' ENTRANCE.

The usual crowd of fight fans were there, forty deep. None of them gave me a look; they had their eyes on the big, wide-shouldered Tunneys and Louises and Marcianos, and the hammed-up Herkys and Tarzans in their flashy costumes and big smiles, with their handlers herding them along like tugs nudging liners into dock. The gateman put out a hand to stop me when I started through the turnstile.

"It's me, Harley. Barney Ramm," I said. A couple of harness cops were standing a few feet away, looking things over. "Let me through; I'm late."

"Hah? Barney—"

"Keep it quiet; I'm a surprise."

"Where'd you dig up that outfit? On a used-Servo lot?" He looked me over like an inspector rejecting a wormy side of mutton. "What is it, a gag?"

"It's a long story. I'll tell it to you sometime. Right now, how's about loaning me a temporary tag? I left my ID in my other pants."

"You pugs," he muttered, but he handed over the pass. I grabbed it.

"Where's Lou Mitch, the starter?" I asked him.

"Try the Registry Office."

I shoved through a crowd of weigh-in men, service techs and arena officials, spotted Lou talking to a couple of trainers. I went over and grabbed his arm.

"It's me, Mitch, Barney Ramm. Listen, where's Gully? I need—"

"Ramm, you bum! Where you been? Where'd you pick up that hulk you got on? Who you think you are, missing the press weigh-in? Get downstairs on the double and dress out! You got twenty minutes, and if you're late, so help me, I'll see you busted out of the fight game!"

"Wha—who, me? Hold it, Lou, I'm not going out there in this condition! I just came down to—"

"Oh, a holdup for more dough, huh? Well, you can work that one out with the promoter and the commissioner. All I know is, you got a contract, and I've got you billed for nineteen minutes from now!"

I started backing away, shaking my head. "Wait a minute, Lou—"

He jerked his head at a couple of the trainers that were listening in. "Grab him and take him down to his stall and get him into his gear! Hustle it!"

I put up a brisk resistance, but it was all wasted effort. Ten minutes later I was standing in the chute, strapped into harness with knots tied in the straps for fit and a copy of the "Afternoon Late Racing Special" padding my helmet up off my ears, listening to the mob in the stands up above, yelling for the next kill. Me.

7

They can talk all they want about how sensitive and responsive a good Servo is, but there's nothing like flesh and blood for making you know you're in trouble.

My heart was kicking hard enough to jar the championship medal on my chest. My mouth was as dry as yesterday's cinnamon toast. I thought about making a fast getaway over the barrier fence, but there was nobody outside who'd be glad to see me except the cops; besides which, I had a mace in my right hand and a fighting net in the left, and after all, I was Barney Ramm the champ. I'd always said it was the man inside the Servo, not the equipment that counted. Tonight I had a chance to prove it—or a kind of a chance; an Org up against a fighting Servo wasn't exactly an even match.

But hell, when was it ever even? The whole fight game was controlled, from top to bottom, by a few sharpies like J. J. Malone. Nobody had ever slipped me the word to take a dive yet, but I'd stretched plenty of bouts to make 'em look good. After all, the fans paid good creds to see two fine-tuned fighting machines pound each other to scrap under the lights. An easy win was taboo. Well, they'd get an unexpected bonus tonight when I got hit and something besides hydraulic fluid ran out.

And then the blast of the bugles caught me like a bucket of ice water and the gate jumped up and I was striding through, head up, trying to look as arrogant as a hunting tiger under the glare of the polyarcs, but feeling very small and very breakable and wondering why I hadn't stayed in that nice safe jail while I had the chance. Out across the spread of the arena the bleachers rose up dark under the high late-evening sky streaked with long pink clouds that looked as remote as fairyland. And under the pooled lights, a big husky Servo was taking his bows, swirling his cloak.

He was too far away, over beyond the raised disk of the Circle, for me to be sure, but it looked like he was picking a heavy-duty prod and nothing else. Maybe the word had gone out that I was in Org, or maybe he was good.

Then he tossed the cape to a handler and came to meet me, sizing me up on the way through the slit in his mask.

Maybe he was wondering what I had up my sleeve. If he was in on the fix, he'd be surprised to see me at all. He'd been expecting a last-minute sub or just a straight default. If not, he'd been figuring on me wearing my Big Charley packed with all the booster gear the law allows. Instead, all he saw was an ordinary-looking five-foot-eleven frame with medium-fair shoulders and maybe just a shade too much padding at the belt line.

The boys back at Files had done right by me, I had to admit. The old Org was in better shape than when I'd filed it, over a year ago. I felt strong, tough and light on my feet; I could feel the old fighting edge coming on. Maybe it was just a false lift from the stuff the techs had loaded me full of, and maybe it was just an animal's combat instinct, an item they hadn't been able to dream up an accessory to imitate. Whatever it was, it was nice to have.

I reached the concrete edge of the Fighting Circle and stepped up on it and was looking across at the other fellow, only fifty feet away and now looking bigger than a Bolo Combat Unit. With the mask I wasn't sure, but he looked like a modified Norge Atlas. He was running through a fancy twirl routine with the prod, and the crowd was eating it up.

There was no law that said I had to wait for him to finish. I slid the mace down to rest solid in my palm with the thong riding tight above my wrist and gave the two-foot club a couple of practice swings. So much for the warm-up. I flipped the net out into casting position with my left hand and moved in on him.

It wasn't like wearing a Servo; I could feel sweat running down my face and the air sighing in my lungs and the blood pumping through my muscles and veins. It was kind of a strange *alive* feeling—as if there were nothing between me and the sky and the earth and I was part of them and they were part of me. A funny feeling. A dangerous, unprotected feeling—but somehow not entirely a bad feeling.

He finished up the ham act when I was ten feet from him, swung to face me. He knew I was there, all right; he was just playing it cool. Swell. While he was playing, I'd take him.

I feinted with the net, then dived in, swung the mace, missed him by half an inch as he back-pedaled. I followed him close, working the club, keeping the net cocked. He backed, looking me over.

"Ramm—is that you in that getup?" he barked.

"Naw—I couldn't make it, so I sent my cousin Julius."

"What happened, you switch brands? Looks like you must of got cut-rate merchandise." He ducked a straight cut and whipped the prod around in a jab that would have paralyzed my neuro center if he'd connected.

"New secret model a big outfit's trying out under wraps," I told him.

He made a fast move, and a long, slim rod I hadn't seen before whipped out and slapped me under the ribs. For a split second I froze. He had me, I was finished. A well-handled magnetic resonator could de-Gauss every microtape in a Servo—and his placement was perfect.

But nothing happened. There was a little tingle, that was all.

Then I got it. I wasn't wearing a Servo—and magnets didn't bother an Org.

The Atlas was looking as confused as I was. He took an extra half-second recovering. That was almost enough. I clipped him across the thigh as he almost fell getting back. He tried with the switch again, sawed it across my chest. I let him; he might as well tickle me with a grass stem. This time I got the net out, snarled his left arm, brought the mace around and laid a good one across his hip. It staggered him, but he managed to spin out, flip the net clear.

"What kind of shielding you got anyway, Ramm?" the Atlas growled. He held the rod out in front of his face, crossed his eyes at it, shook it hard and made one more try. I let him come in under my guard, and the shaft slid along my side as if he were trying to wipe it clean on my shirt. While he was busy with that, I dropped the net, got a two-handed grip on the mace, brought it around in a flat arc and laid a solid wallop right where it would do him the most good—square on the hip joint.

I heard the socket go. He tried to pivot on his good leg, tottered and just managed to stay on his feet, swearing. I came in fast and just got a glimpse of the electro-prod coming up. Concentrating on the magnetic rod, I'd forgotten the other. I tried to check and slide off to the right, but all of a sudden blinding blue lights were popping all over the sky. Something came up and hit me alongside the head, and then I was doing slow somersaults through pretty purple clouds, trying hard to figure which side was up. Then the pain hit. For a couple of seconds I scraped at my chest, reaching for circuit breakers that weren't there. Then I got mad.

It was as if all of a sudden, nothing could stop me. The Atlas was a target, and all I wanted was just to reach it. If there was a mountain in the way, I'd pick it up and throw it over my shoulder. A charging elephant would be a minor nuisance. I could even stand up, unassisted—if I tried hard enough.

I got the feel of something solid under my hands, groped and found some more of it with my feet, pushed hard and blinked away the fog to see the Atlas just making it back onto his good leg. I had to rest awhile then, on all fours. He stooped to twiddle a reset for emergency power to the damaged joint, then started for me, hopping hard enough to shake the ground. A little voice told me to wait. . . .

He stopped, swung the prod up, and I rolled, grabbed his good leg, twisted with everything I had. It wasn't enough. He hopped, jabbed with the prod, missed, and I was on my feet now, feeling like I'd been skinned and soaked in brine. My breath burned my throat like a blowtorch, and all around the crowd roar was like a tidal wave rolling across a sinking continent.

I backed, and he followed. I tried to figure the time until the pit stop, but I didn't know how long I'd been out here; I didn't have a timer ticking under my left ear, keeping me posted. And now the Atlas was on to what was going on. I knew that, when he reached for the show-knife strapped to his left hip. Against a Servo, that particular tool was useless, but he could let the cool night air into an Org's gizzard with it, and he knew it.

Then my foot hit the edge of the paved circle and I went down, flat on my back on the sand.

The Atlas came after me, and I scrambled back, got to my feet just in time. The knife blade hissed through the air just under my chin.

"You've had it, Ramm," the Atlas said, and swung again. I tried to get the club up for a counterblow but it was too heavy. I let it drop and drag in the sand. Through the dust cloud we were making, I saw the Atlas fumbling with his control buttons. Tears welled up in his eyes, sluiced down over his face. He didn't like the dust any better than I did. Maybe not as well. . . .

I felt an idea pecking at its shell; a dirty idea, but better than none.

The mace was dangling by its thong. I slipped it free, threw it at him; it clanged off his knees and I stooped, came up with a handful of fine sand and as he closed in threw it straight into his face.

The effect was striking. His eyes turned to mud pockets. I stepped aside, and he went right past me, making swipes at the air with the big sticker, and I swung in behind him and tilted another handful down inside his neckband. I could hear it grate in the articulated rib armor as he came around.

"Ramm, you lousy little—" I took aim and placed a nice gob square in his vocabulary. He backed off, pumping emergency air to clear the pipes, spouting dust like Mount Aetna, but I knew I had him. The mouth cavity on just about every Servo in the market was a major lube duct; he had enough grit in his gears to stop a Continental Siege Unit. But his mouth was still open, so I funneled in another double handful.

He stopped, locked his knee joints and concentrated on his

problem. That gave me my opening to reach out and switch his main circuit breaker off.

He froze. I waited half a minute for the dust to clear, while the crowd roar died away to a kind of confused buzzing, like robbed bees.

Then I reached out, put a finger against his chest, and shoved—just gently. He leaned back, teetered for a second, and toppled over stiff as a lamppost. You could hear the thud all the way to the student bleachers. I held on for another ten seconds, just to make it look good, then kneeled over on top of him.

8

". . . but I was too late." Gully Fishbein's voice was coming up out of a barrel, a barrel full of thick molasses syrup somebody had dumped me into. I opened my mouth to complain and a noise like glug came out.

"He's awake!" Gully yelped. I started to deny it, but the effort was too much.

"Barney, I tried to catch you, but you were already out there." Gully sounded indignant. "Cripes, kid, you should of known I wouldn't let 'em railroad you!"

"Don't worry about Ramm." A breezy voice jostled Gully's aside. "Boy, this is the story of the decade! You figure to go up against a Servo again in Org, when you get out of the shop—I mean hospital? How did it feel to take five thousand volts of DC? You know the experts say it should have killed you. It would have knocked out any Servo on the market—"

"Nix, Baby!" Gully elbowed his way back in again. "My boy's gotta rest. And you can tell the world the Combo's out of business. Now anybody can afford to fight. Me and Barney have put the game back in the hands of the people."

"Yeah! The sight of that Atlas, out on its feet—and Ramm here, in Org, yet, with one finger . . ."

I unglued an eyelid and blinked at half a dozen fuzzy faces like custard pies floating around me.

"We'll talk contract with you, Fishbein," somebody said.

". . . .call for some new regulations," somebody said.

"——dred thousand cees, first network rights."

". . . era of the Servo in the arena is over. . . ."

". . . hear what Malone says about this. Wow!"

"Malone," I heard my voice say, like a boot coming out of mud. "The cr . . . crook. It was him . . . put the Sullivan . . . up to it. . . ."

"Up to nothing, Barney." Gully was bending over me. "That was J.J. hisself in that Servo! And here's the payoff. He registered the satisfaction in his own name—and of course, every fighter in his stable is acting in his name, legally. So when you met Mysterious Marvin and knocked him on his duff you satisfied his claim. You're in the clear, kid. You can relax. There's nothing to worry about."

"Oh, Barney!" It was a new voice, a nice soft little squeal of a girl voice. A neat little Org face with a turned-up nose zeroed in on me, with a worried look in the big brown eyes.

"Julie! Where—I mean, how . . . ?"

"I was there, Barney. I see all your fights, even if—even if I don't approve. And today—oh, Barney, you were so brave, so marvelous, out there alone, against that machine. . . ." She sighed and nestled her head against my shoulder.

"Gully," I said. "Exactly how long have I got to stay in this place?"

"The Servo-tech—I mean the doc—says a week anyway."

"Set up a wedding for a week from today."

Julie jumped and stared at me.

"Oh, Barney! But you—you know what I said . . . about those zombies. . . ."

"I know."

"But, Barney . . ." Gully didn't know whether to cry or grin. "You mean . . . ?"

"Sell my Servos," I said. "The whole wardrobe. My days of being a pair of TV eyes peeking out of a walking dummy and kidding myself I'm alive are over."

"Yeah, but Barney—a guy with your ideas about what's fun—like skiing, and riding the jetboards, and surfing, and sky-diving—you can't take the risks! You only got the one Org body!"

"I found out a couple of things out there tonight, Gully. It takes a live appetite to make a meal a feast. From now on, whatever I do, it'll be *me* doing it. Clocking records is okay, I guess, but there's some things that it takes an Org to handle."

"Like what?" Gully yelled, and went on with a lot more in the same vein. I wasn't listening, though. I was too busy savoring a pair of warm, soft, *live* lips against mine.

ROBERT B. SILVERBERG AND RANDALL GARRETT

A dozen Earthmen stuck on a remote planet somewhere back of subspace, with absolutely nothing interesting to do . . . it's a situation guaranteed to lead to trouble for someone, probably the Earthmen. Especially when they start racing animals they know nothing about, and betting on the outcome.

Robert Silverberg and Randall Garrett wrote many stories together in the 1950's, but this one, originally published under an obscure pen name and never before reprinted, will be new even to their most rabid fans.

The Great
Kladnar Race

I don't know whose idea it was to hold the *kladnar* race.
There were twelve of us in that miserable trading post on Gornik
VII, all sweating out the year that would have to pass before we
could apply for transfers to some less deadly dull planet.

There wasn't much action on Gornik VII—so we manufactured some. It happened one morning, as the bunch of us were
sitting outside the Terran encampment, waiting boredly for the
natives to show up with their produce.

Someone—I wish I knew who it was—pointed to the
galumphing form of a *kladnar* approaching in the distance, and
said, "Hey! I've got a great idea! Why don't we organize a
kladnar race?"

I remember the idea amused me tremendously. If you
haven't ever seen a tridim of a *kladnar*, you've never seen one of
the silliest-looking beasts that ever infested an alien world.
They're long and low-slung, with six knob-ended, spindly legs,
and broad backs that would be marvelous for carrying passen-
gers or cargo, if it weren't for the ridge of spines running along
them. The natives use the *kladnars* as beasts of burden—they
don't mind sitting on the spines, it seems—and every morning
we were accustomed to seeing a dozen or more purple-and-
green *kladnars* stabled at our outpost while their masters hag-
gled with us over the exchange value of some trinket or gewgaw.

Within a few minutes, we were huddled together in an
excited group, discussing the project. At last, something to take
the curse of boredom from Gornik VII!

"We can set up a toteboard," Hamilton said. "Lord knows we've got plenty of loose cash!"

"Should we get out a *Racing Form*?" asked Demaret waggishly. "And who'll print the scorecards?"

Lieutenant Davis stared out at the plain before us. "We can hold the race out there," he said. "A two-mile course, straightaway. There's room for a dozen *kladnars* to run, easily.

"Will the natives lend us the animals?" I asked.

Davis nodded. "They won't mind. It'll be a novelty for them, too."

"It ought to be something," Willis said.

The Great *Kladnar* Race became the biggest thing the insignificant world of Gornik VII had experienced since the day Earthmen had first landed there.

The natives—small, furry humanoids who were friendly and cooperative at all times—took to the race with great enthusiasm, once we explained what it was all about.

Gummun Lugal, the local chieftain, was the man we had to get it across to.

He frowned, wrinkling his furry brow. "I don't quite understand. You want to borrow *kladnars* and let them run in that field?"

I nodded. "That's right."

"But—*why*?"

"It's a sport we Earthmen enjoy. We start all the *kladnars* from the same place, and let them run toward another given place. Then we bet money on which *kladnar* will get there first."

"Bet?" Gummun Lugal said, in hopeless confusion. "What is that?"

"I mean," I said, "that each of us puts down a certain sum of money to support the *kladnar* of his choice. Then the man who backed the winning *kladnar* collects some of the other men's money."

"I think I understand," the alien said dimly. "Go through it once again, will you?"

I outlined the scheme to him a second time. Comprehension

finally broke through his small brain, and he nodded happily. "I see! I see! It is a game, you might say."

"You might say indeed," I said.

"The twelve *kladnars* will be ready whenever you want them," the chieftain said.

We swung into activity with an enthusiasm you'd hardly expect from twelve Earthmen stuck on a backwater planet. We measured off a two-mile course, built a starting gate, chalked in a finish line. Our radio tech cooked up a photo-timer in case of a close heat. We decorated the racing grounds with bright-colored cloth from our endless stock of trading goods, cutting out banners and streamers galore. It looked just like home by the time we were finished.

The day of the race, the natives started filing into the stands we had erected, and old Gummun Lugal and some of his sons came galumphing in riding a dozen *kladnars*, which they brought around back to our tent.

We equipped each one with a silk of a different color, with a large number emblazoned on it, and the native jockeys each had an armband of the same color. An armband was the best we could do, since they wouldn't wear anything else.

The day before, we had looked over the twelve *kladnars* they were supplying. Each of us had a chance to go down the row, peering at teeth and forepaws, trying to judge the things. We had no record of previous performances, of course. The *kladnars* were simply beasts of burden, not racing animals. It was a familiar sight on Gornik VII to see a long string of them trudging along Indian file carrying bundles of goods. So we had to guess which one might be the fastest. There was no sure thing.

Naturally, we kept our conclusions to ourselves. I picked Number 5 myself, a sturdy-looking animal with a glint of fierce determination in his eye. He seemed a sure thing to come through first, since the rest of the *kladnars*, it seemed to me, were much sadder creatures—and one of them, Number 9, was so decrepit-looking that I was sure he'd drop dead after the first furlong.

Computer technician Flaherty dragged his small Mark VII

job out of the ship and set it up at the track, and radio tech Dombrowski hooked the computer to a videoscreen to make an improvised parimutuel board.

We opened a betting window. Lieutenant Davis stood behind it and took the money, while the crowds of natives watched with keen interest from the stands. All eleven of us lined up, credit-pieces in hand, to bet.

"Four credits on Number Three," Demaret said.

"I'll put my dough on Number Seven," said Dombrowski.

"Mine's Number Six," said Willis.

"Same here," said Flaherty, and the two Irishmen glared unhappily at each other. Naturally, two bets on the same *kladnar* reduced the possible winnings on the creature.

"I'll take Five," I said.

The odds on the screen flickered and changed with each bet. When we were all through, I glanced up at the board to see how things stood.

Three *kladnars* led the list at 12 to 1. No one at all had put money on numbers 2, 4, or 9, and they rated as longshots. From there the odds trailed away. My *kladnar*, Number 5, had proved popular; I stood to pick up only a couple of credits in the event of a win.

"Okay," Lieutenant Davis said. "The bets are all in. Let's get the race under way."

"One moment, please," said a thin voice. We all glanced down in surprise, and saw the small form of Chieftain Gummun Lugal. He elbowed his way to the betting window and peered up at the lieutenant.

"What is it?" Davis asked.

"We'd like to know," the chieftain asked hesitantly, "if it's all right for our people to place bets too."

Davis frowned. "You want to bet?"

Gummun Lugal nodded.

We held a hasty conference outside the window. "Why not?" I said. "Their money's good, isn't it? And it increases the total kitty tremendously."

"It confuses things, though," Demaret objected. "If we mix their money and ours—"

"We can equalize it later," Davis said. "I think it's a good idea to let them bet."

So did the rest of us, and we told Gummun Lugal that it was all right. He turned and yelled something to the stands, and what looked like an endless stream of aliens descended from the bleachers and formed a long line in front of the betting window.

Fifteen minutes later, we were very worried indeed.

I stared up at the parimutuel board. "They're all betting on Number Nine," I said. "Every last one of them! And Number Nine's a dog. It'll keel over before the race can start."

"If it does we'll be lucky," Davis said. "If Nine should win we'll have to pay out a fortune, even with the odds as low as they are."

Demaret scowled. "There's something funny going on. There must be some reason why the natives are all going for the same kladnar. You think the race is fixed?"

"I don't know," the lieutenant said. "Let's go see Gummun Lugal again."

We ringed ourselves around the chieftain and Davis said, "Gummun Lugal, we want to make a change in the nature of the race."

"Lieutenant?"

"We want to change things a little bit. Instead of having your people ride the kladnars, we'll be the jockeys."

The chieftain was silent for a moment, and Davis added, "If you won't agree to that, we'll have to call off the race."

Immediately he begged us to reconsider. "No, no, we'll be deeply honored to have the Earthmen ride our lowly beasts!" he said. "By all means!"

"You don't object?"

"Not at all," Gummun Lugal said.

"Very good. We'll start the race immediately. The board's closed, and no more bets will be accepted."

Davis called us together. "All right, men. We're going to ride these beasts ourselves, and we're going to ride them fairly. I'll assign you to mounts at random, and if you happen to be riding the wrong horse, ride it as if you've got your pension bet on it. We can't afford to look dishonest in front of these natives."

Dombrowski raised his hand. "Fine, sir—but I have a suggestion. Suppose you let me ride Number Nine—just as a precautionary measure?" The radio tech patted his three-hundred pound girth and chuckled. "I may slow the beast up a bit, you know."

"Go ahead," Davis said. "The rest of you take these slips of paper, and get aboard. We've got to get the race going."

I drew Number 3. Demaret, who had bet on 3, smiled and said, "Give her a run, will you? I've got four credits riding on her tail."

"Don't worry," I said. "I'll be in there all the way." I glanced over at Number 5, and saw Lieutenant Davis climbing aboard. *Make it a good run, Lieutenant*, I thought silently.

But I didn't intend to hold Number 3 back. I'd ride it with all I had, even if it meant beating out my own horse in a photo finish.

I climbed aboard 3 and guided it slowly to the starting gate. The course was a two-mile straightaway, and so position didn't much matter. Next to me, Dombrowski sat athwart poor bedraggled old 9, carrying with him the hopes —and cash—of the whole native village.

Since all twelve of us were needed to ride, Davis handed the starting gun to Gummun Lugal and told him what to do.

I grabbed the reins.

"Go!"

The shot resounded loudly and we were off. My *kladnar* broke badly, and I found myself in the back almost at once. To my horror, I saw Dombrowski and Number 9 several paces in the lead.

I urged my mount on. It wasn't pleasant, riding that beast. The row of blunt three-inch spines down its wide back didn't make for a pleasant cushion, and its six spindly legs went up and down like a set of out-of-phase pistons. I knew I was going to get awfully seasick before the race was over.

"Giddyap!" I yelled, not knowing an appropriate command for a *kladnar*. And, gradually, my animal started to move. I

passed into the bunched pack, threaded past, emerged neck and
neck with Lieutenant Davis aboard 5 and Demaret on 7. The
Kladnars weren't moving at much more than a fast crawl, and I
turned to wave at Davis as I pushed past.

His face was set in a grim line. He gestured up ahead, and I
gasped.

Old Number 9 was ten paces ahead, jogging along
placidly, without worrying about Dombrowski's bulk in the
slightest. The race was coming to the halfway point— and
Number 9 was in the lead!

Let's go, boy!" I crooned. My mount edged past Number 7,
then past my own favorite, 3. *Good-bye, sweet money,* I
thought. I knew it was up to me to catch Number 9.

I could see the ancient beast plodding along just ahead. He
wasn't moving very quickly—but my own mount was going
even more slowly. I thudded my heels into the *kladnar's* side,
tired to urge him onward.

No soap. I got up within about two paces of Number 9 and
then my *kladnar* fell into an obliging trot. It was lickety-split,
lickety-split, all the way to the finish line. Dombrowski and
Number 9 crossed first. I came over right after to place.

I turned and looked back. The other ten *kladnars* were
stretched out in a long line.

The crowd was roaring. I thought of the cash we'd have to
pay out to cover thos hundreds of bets on Number 9, and felt
sick.

It took nearly two hours to pay off all the natives. They
hadn't bet much individually, but there were a hell of a lot of
them.

We had to pay them, naturally. It wasn't only a matter of
honor; the company would have raised holy hell if we'd
welshed on our bets and lost face to the local populace.

We exhausted our own kitty pretty quickly. We'd made the
damn fool mistake of guaranteeing a profit, so we had to pay out
more than we took in. When our own money was gone, we had to
dig into company money. Luckily, it held out to the end. We

were bankrupt and in debt to our employers, but we'd paid off on the race.

Gummun Lugal was near the betting window as Lieutenant Davis sourly paid out the bets. He kept bobbing his head and smiling, showing his toothy rust-red smile. "What wonderful men you Earthmen are!" he cried. "Distributing all this wealth to us!"

"It's not our idea," I said. My voice must have sounded surly, because the old chieftain's smile faded.

"But—I—I don't understand—"

"Look here, Gummun Lugal," I said, trying to keep from sounding too nasty, "just how in blazes did all your people know that Number Nine was going to win? That decrepit old creature couldn't outrun a man with two broken legs."

His eyes widened in utter astonishment. "You mean—you didn't know? But—"

"What is this? How did you cheat us? And why?" I was really boiling and it took every bit of self-control I had to keep my voice even.

"Cheat? Why, no. We thought you were well aware that Number Nine was the lead animal of the caravan."

"*Caravan?*" My voice must have cracked there; it sounded like a parrot-screech. "You gave us a trained caravan team?"

He smiled happily. "Of course. Otherwise they would not have run together. Unless they are trained together, the *kladnar* will shy away from each other and fight."

"And Number Nine was the lead animal?"

"Oh, yes. We think it was a fine race. It showed the training of the animals. Yes; a very fine race. We must try to run another sometime."

I turned away. "Sure. As soon as Hades freezes over, we'll let you know. We'll have another race then."

"Thank you. It was fine of you; very fine."

It was very plain now. The caravan teams were trained to follow each other in a certain order—or else. No *kladnar* would have gone against his lifelong training and tried to pass his leader.

It cost us more than mere money to pay off that race; we lost our transfers, because we had to stay on Gornik VII an extra year to make up our losses.

We managed not to get bored, though. We didn't run any more *kladnar* races.

And I wish I could remember who the bum was who thought of the idea in the first place!

CLIFFORD D. SIMAK

Here's another previously "undiscovered"
story, a delightful novelette by the famous au-
thor of *City, Way Station,* and 120 more
science-fiction tales. How it could have been
overlooked seems unexplainable till you remember that it originally appeared in 1943 in
a pulp magazine that's now very rare.

So now you have a chance to meet Mr. Oliver
Meek, ex-bookkeeper for Lunar Exports now
traveling in the wilds of the solar
system . . . and meeting some *very* wild people, who insist that he teach them how to
play space polo. Don't worry if you don't
know how space polo is played—neither
does Mr. Meek. . . .

Mr. Meek
Plays Polo

I

The sign read:

ATOMIC MOTORS REPAIRED
BUSTED PLATES PATCHED UP
ROCKET TUBES RELINED
WHEEZE IN, WHIZ OUT!

It added, as an afterthought, in shaky, inexpert lettering:

WE FIX ANYTHING

Mr. Oliver Meek stared owlishly at the sign, which hung from an arm attached to a metal standard sunk in solid rock. A second sign was wired to the standard just below the metal arm, but its legend was faint, almost illegible. Meek blinked at it through thick-lensed spectacles, finally deciphered its scrawl:

ASK ABOUT EDUCATED BUGS

A bit bewildered, but determined not to show it, Meek swung away from the signpost and gravely regarded the settlement. On the chart it was indicated by a fairly sizable dot, but that was merely a matter of comparison. Out Saturn-way even the tiniest outpost assumes importance far beyond its size.

The slab of rock was no more than five miles across, perhaps even less. Here, in its approximate center, were two buildings, both of almost identical construction, semispherical and metal. Out here, Meek realized, shelter was the thing. Architecture merely for architecture's sake was still a long way off.

One of the buildings was the repair shop which the sign advertised. The other, according to the crudely painted legend smeared above its entrance lock, was the Saturn Inn.

The rest of the rock was landing field, pure and simple. Blasters had leveled off the humps and irregularities so spaceships could set down.

Two ships now were on the field, pulled up close against the repair shop. One, Meek noticed, belonged to the Solar Health and Welfare Department, the other to the Galactic Pharmaceutical Corporation. The Galactic ship was a freighter, ponderous and slow. It was here, Meek knew, to take on a cargo of radiation moss. But the other was a puzzler. Meek wrinkled his brow and blinked his eyes, trying to figure out what a welfare ship would be doing in this remote corner of the solar system.

Slowly and carefully, Meek clumped toward the squat repair shop. Once or twice he stumbled, hoping fervently he wouldn't get the feet of his cumbersome spacesuit all tangled up. The gravity was slight, next to nonexistent, and one who wasn't used to it had to take things easy and remember where he was.

Behind him Saturn filled a tenth of the sky, a yellow, lemon-tinged ball, streaked here and there with faint crimson lines and blotched with angry, bright green patches.

To right and left glinted the whirling, twisting, tumbling rocks that made up the Inner Ring, while arcing above the horizon opposed to Saturn were the spangled glistening rainbows of the other rings.

"Like dewdrops in the black of space," Meek mumbled to himself. But he immediately felt ashamed of himself for growing poetic. This sector of space, he knew, was not in the least poetic. It was hard and savage, and as he thought about that, he hitched up his gun belt and struck out with a firmer tread that almost upset him. After that, he tried to think of nothing except keeping his two feet under him.

Reaching the repair shop's entrance lock, he braced himself solidly to keep his balance, reached out and pressed a buzzer. Swiftly the lock spun outward and a moment later Meek had passed through the entrance vault and stepped into the office.

A dungareed mechanic sat tilted in a chair against a wall, feet on the desk, a greasy cap pushed back on his head.

Meek stamped his feet gratefully, pleased at feeling Earth gravity under him again. He lifted the hinged helmet of his suit back on his shoulders.

"You are the gentleman who can fix things?" he asked the mechanic.

The mechanic stared. Here was no hell-for-leather freighter pilot, no bewhiskered roamer of the outer orbits. Meek's hair was white and stuck out in uncombed tufts in a dozen directions. His skin was pale. His blue eyes looked watery behind the thick lenses that rode his nose. Even the bulky spacesuit failed to hide his stooped shoulders and slight frame.

The mechanic said nothing.

Meek tried again. "I saw the sign. It said you could fix anything. So I . . ."

The mechanic shook himself.

"Sure," he agreed, still slightly dazed. "Sure I can fix you up. What you got?"

He swung his feet off the desk.

"I ran into a swarm of pebbles," Meek confessed. "Not much more than dust, really, but the screen couldn't stop it all."

He fumbled his hands self-consciously. "Awkward of me," he said.

"It happens to the best of them," the mechanic consoled. "Saturn sweeps in clouds of the stuff. Thicker than hell when you reach the Rings. Lots of ships pull in with punctures. Won't take no time."

Meek cleared his throat uneasily. "I'm afraid it's more than a puncture. A pebble got into the instruments. Washed out some of them."

The mechanic clucked sympathetically. "You're lucky. Tough job to bring in a ship without all the instruments. Must have a honey of a navigator."

"I haven't got a navigator," Meek said quietly.

The mechanic stared at him, eyes popping. "You mean you brought it in alone? No one with you?"

Meek gulped and nodded. "Dead reckoning," he said.

The mechanic glowed with sudden admiration. "I don't know who you are, mister," he declared, "but whoever you are, you're the best damn pilot that ever took to space."

"Really I'm not," said Meek. "I haven't done much piloting, you see. Up until just a while ago, I never had left Earth. Book-keeper for Lunar Exports."

"Bookkeeper!" yelped the mechanic. "How come a book-keeper can handle a ship like that?"

"I learned it," said Meek.

"You learned it?"

"Sure, from a book. I saved my money and I studied. I always wanted to see the solar system and here I am."

Dazedly, the mechanic took off his greasy cap, laid it care-fully on the desk, reached out for a spacesuit that hung from a wall hook.

"Afraid this might take a while," he said. "Especially if we have to wait for parts. Have to get them in from Titan City. Why don't you go over to the Inn. Tell Moe I sent you. They'll treat you right."

"Thank you," said Meek, "but there's something else I'm wondering about. There was another sign out there. Something about educated bugs."

"Oh, them," said the mechanic. "They belong to Gus Hamil-ton. Maybe 'belong' ain't the right word because they were on the rock before Gus took over. Anyhow, Gus is mighty proud of them, although at times they sure run him ragged. First year they almost drove him loopy trying to figure out what kind of game they were playing."

"Game?" asked Meek, wondering if he was being hoaxed.

"Sure, game. Like checkers. Only it ain't. Not chess, neither. Even worse than that. Bugs dig themselves a batch of holes, then choose up sides and play for hours. About the time Gus would think he had it figured out, they'd change the rules and throw him off again."

"That doesn't make sense," protested Meek.

"Stranger," declared the mechanic, solemnly, "there ain't nothing about them bugs that makes sense. Gus's rock is the only one they're on. Gus thinks maybe the rock don't even belong to the solar system. Thinks maybe it's a hunk of stone from some other solar system. Figures maybe it crossed space somehow and was captured by Saturn, sucked into the Ring. That would explain why it's the only one that has the bugs. They come along with it, see."

"This Gus Hamilton," said Meek. "I'd like to see him. Where could I find him?"

"Go over to the Inn and wait around," advised the mechanic. "He'll come in sooner or later. Drops around regular, except when his rheumatism bothers him, to pick up a bundle of papers. Subscribes to a daily paper, he does. Only man out here that does any reading. But all he reads is the sports section. Nuts about sports, Gus is."

II

Moe, bartender at Saturn Inn, leaned his elbow on the bar and braced his chin in an outspread palm. His face wore a melancholy, hang-dog look. Moe liked things fairly peaceable, but now he saw trouble coming in big batches.

"Lady," he declared mournfully, "you sure picked yourself a job. The boys around here don't take to being uplifted and improved. They ain't worth it, either. Just ring-rats, that's all they are."

Henrietta Perkins, representative for the public health and welfare department of the Solar government, shuddered at his suggestion of anything so low it didn't yearn for betterment.

"But those terrible feuds," she protested. "Fighting just because they live in different parts of the Ring. It's natural they might feel some rivalry, but all this killing! Surely they don't enjoy getting killed."

"Sure they enjoy it," declared Moe. "Not being killed, maybe . . . although they're willing to take a chance on that. Not many of them get killed, in fact. Just a few that get sort of careless. But even if some of them are killed, you can't go messing around with that feud of theirs. If them boys out in Sectors Twenty-Three and Thirty-Seven didn't have their feud they'd plain die of boredom. They just got to have somebody to fight with. They been fighting, off and on, for years."

"But they could fight with something besides guns," said the welfare lady, a-smirk with righteousness. "That's why I'm here. To try to get them to turn their natural feelings of rivalry into less deadly and disturbing channels. Direct their energies into other activities."

"Like what?" asked Moe, fearing the worst.

"Athletic events," said Miss Perkins.

"Tin shinny, maybe," suggested Moe, trying to be sarcastic.

She missed the sarcasm. "Or spelling contests," she said.

"Them fellows can't spell," insisted Moe.

"Games of some sort, then. Competitive games."

"Now you're talking," Moe enthused. "They take to games. Seven-toed Pete with the deuces wild."

The inner door of the entrance lock grated open and a space-suited figure limped into the room. The spacesuit visor snapped up and a brush of gray whiskers sprouted into view.

It was Gus Hamilton.

He glared at Moe. "What in tarnation is all this foolishness?" he demanded. "Got your message, I did, and here I am. But it better be important."

He hobbled to the bar. Moe reached for a bottle and shoved it toward him, keeping out of reach.

"Have some trouble?" he asked, trying to be casual.

"Trouble! Hell, yes!" blustered Gus. "But I ain't the only one that's going to have trouble. Somebody sneaked over and stole the injector out of my space crate. Had to borrow Hank's to get over here. But I know who it was. There ain't but one other ring-rat got a rocket my injector will fit."

"Bud Craney," said Moe. It was no secret. Every man in the two sectors of the Ring knew just exactly what kind of spacecraft the other had.

"That's right," said Gus, "and I'm fixing to go over into Thirty-Seven and yank Bud up by the roots."

He took a jolt of liquor. "Yes, sir, I sure aim to crucify him."

His eyes lighted on Miss Henrietta Perkins.

"Visitor?" he asked.

"She's from the government," said Moe.

"Revenuer?"

"Nope. From the welfare outfit. Aims to help you fellows out. Says there ain't no sense in you boys in Twenty-Three all the time fighting with the gang from Thirty-Seven."

Gus stared in disbelief.

Moe tried to be helpful. "She wants you to play games."

Gus strangled on his drink, clawed for air, wiped his eyes.

"So that's why you asked me over here. Another of your danged peace parleys. Come and talk things over, you said. So I came."

"There's something in what she says," defended Moe. "You ring-rats been ripping up space for a long time now. Time you growed up and settled down. You're aiming on going over right now and pulverizing Bud. It won't do you any good."

"I'll get a heap of satisfaction out of it," insisted Gus. "And, besides, I'll get my injector back. Might even take a few things off Bud's ship. Some of the parts on mine are wearing kind of thin."

Gus took another drink, glowering at Miss Perkins.

"So the government sent you out to make us respectable," he said.

"Merely to help you, Mr. Hamilton," she declared. "To turn your hatreds into healthy competition."

"Games, eh?" said Gus. "Maybe you got something, after all. Maybe we could fix up some kind of game. . . ."

"Forget it, Gus," warned Moe. "If you're thinking of energy guns at fifty paces, it's out. Miss Perkins won't stand for anything like that."

Gus wiped his whiskers and looked hurt. "Nothing of the sort," he denied. "Dang it, you must think I ain't got no sportsmanship at all. I was thinking of a real sport. A game they play back on Earth and Mars. Read about it in my papers. Follow the teams, I do. Always wanted to see a game, but never did."

Miss Perkins beamed. "What game is it, Mr. Hamilton?"

"Space polo," said Gus.

"Why, how wonderful," simpered Miss Perkins. "And you boys have the spaceships to play it with."

Moe looked alarmed. "Miss Perkins," he warned, "don't let him talk you into it."

"You shut your trap," snapped Gus. "She wants us to play games, don't she. Well, polo is a game. A nice, respectable game. Played in the best society."

"It wouldn't be no nice, respectable game the way you fellows would play it," predicted Moe. "It would turn into mass murder. Wouldn't be one of you who wouldn't be planning on getting even with someone else, once you got him in the open."

Miss Perkins gasped. "Why, I'm sure they wouldn't!"

"Of course we wouldn't," declared Gus, solemn as an owl.

"And that ain't all," said Moe, warming to the subject. "Those crates you guys got wouldn't last out the first chukker. Most of them would just naturally fall apart the first sharp turn they made. You can't play polo in ships tied up with haywire. Those broomsticks you ring-rats ride around on are so used to second-rate fuel they'd split wide open first squirt of high-test stuff you gave them."

The inner locks grated open and a man stepped through into the room.

"You're prejudiced," Gus told Moe. "You just don't like space polo, that is all. You ain't got no blueblood in you. We'll leave it up to this man here. We'll ask his opinion of it."

The man flipped back his helmet, revealing a head thatched by white hair and dominated by a pair of outsize spectacles.

"My opinion, sir," said Oliver Meek, "seldom amounts to much."

"All we want to know," Gus told him, "is what you think of space polo."

"Space polo," declared Meek, "is a noble game. It requires expert piloting, a fine sense of timing and . . ."

"There, you see!" whooped Gus, triumphantly.

"I saw a game once," Meek volunteered.

"Swell," bellowed Gus. "We'll have you coach our team."

"But," protested Meek, "but . . . but . . ."

"Oh, Mr. Hamilton," exulted Miss Perkins, "you are so wonderful. You think of everything."

"Hamilton!" squeaked Meek.

"Sure," said Gus. "Old Gus Hamilton. Grow the finest dog-gone radiation moss you ever clapped your eyes on."

"Then you're the gentleman who has bugs," said Meek.

"Now, look here," warned Gus, "you watch what you say or I'll hang one on you."

"He means your rock bugs," Moe explained, hastily.

"Oh, them," said Gus.

"Yes," said Meek, "I'm interested in them. I'd like to see them."

"See them," said Gus. "Mister, you can have them if you want them. Drove me out of house and home, they did. They're dippy over metal. Any kind of metal, but alloys especially. Eat the stuff. They'll tromp you to death heading for a spaceship. Got so I had to move over to another rock to live. Tried to fight it out with them, but they whipped me pure and simple. Moved out and let them have the place after they started to eat my shack right out from underneath my feet."

Meek looked crestfallen.

"Can't get near them, then," he said.

"Sure you can," said Gus. "Why not?"

"Well, a spacesuit's metal and . . ."

"Got that all fixed up," said Gus. "You come back with me and I'll let you have a pair of stilts."

"Stilts?"

"Yeah. Wooden stilts. Them danged fool bugs don't know what wood is. Seem to be scared of it, sort of. You can walk right among them if you want to, long as you're walking on the stilts."

Meek gulped. He could imagine what stilt walking would be like in a place where gravity was no more than the faintest whisper.

III

The bugs had dug a new set of holes, much after the manner of a Chinese checkerboard, and now were settling down into their respective places preparatory to the start of another game.

For a mile or more across the flat surface of the rock that was Gus Hamilton's moss garden ran a string of such game-boards, each one different, each one having served as the scene of a now completed game.

Oliver Meek cautiously wedged his stilts into two pitted pockets of rock, eased himself slowly and warily against the face of a knob of stone that jutted from the surface.

Even in his youth, Meek remembered, he never had been any great shakes on stilts. Here, on this bucking, weaving rock, with slick surfaces and practically no gravity, a man had to be an expert to handle them. Meek knew now he was no expert. A half dozen dents in his space armor was ample proof of that.

Comfortably braced against the upjutting of stone, Meek dug into the pouch of his space gear, brought out a notebook and stylus. Flipping the pages, he stared, frowning, at the diagrams that covered them.

None of the diagrams made sense. They showed the patterns of three other boards and the moves that had been made by the bugs in playing out the game. Apparently, in each case, the game had been finished. Which, Meek knew, should have meant that some solution had been reached, some point won, some advantage gained.

But so far as Meek could see from study of the diagrams, there was not even a purpose or a problem, let alone a solution or a point.

The whole thing was squirrely. But, Meek told himself, it fitted in. The whole Saturnian system was wacky. The rings, for example. Debris of a moon smashed up by Saturn's pull? Sweepings of space? No one knew.

Saturn itself, for that matter. A planet that kept man at bay with deadly radiations. But radiations that, while they kept man at a distance, at the same time served man. For here, on the Inner Ring, where they had become so diluted that ordinary space armor filtered them out, they made possible the medical magic of the famous radiation moss.

One of the few forms of plant life found in the cold of space, the moss was nurtured by those mysterious radiations. Planted elsewhere, on kindlier worlds, it wilted and refused to grow. The radiations had been analyzed, Meek knew, and reproduced under laboratory conditions, but there still was something missing, some vital, elusive factor that could not be analyzed. Under the artificial radiation, the moss still wilted and died.

And because Earth needed the moss to cure a dozen maladies, and because it would grow nowhere else but here on the Inner Ring, men squatted on the crazy swirl of spacial boulders that made up the Ring. Men like Hamilton, living on rocks that bucked and heaved along their orbits like chips riding the crest of a raging flood. Men who endured loneliness, dared death when crunching orbits intersected or, when rickety spacecraft flared, who went mad with nothing to do, with the mockery of space before them.

Meek shrugged his shoulders, almost upsetting himself.

The bugs had started the game and Meek craned forward cautiously, watching eagerly, stylus poised above the notebook.

Crawling clumsily, the tiny insectlike creatures moved about, solemnly popping in and out of holes.

If there were opposing sides . . . and if it was a game, there'd have to be . . . they didn't seem to alternate the moves. Although, Meek admitted, certain rules and conditions which he had failed to note or recognize might determine the number and order of moves allowed each side.

Suddenly there was confusion on the board. For a moment a half dozen of the bugs raced madly about, as if seeking the proper hole to occupy. Then, as suddenly, all movement had ceased. And in another moment, they were on the move again, orderly again, but retracing their movements, going back several plays beyond the point of confusion.

Just as one would do when one made a mistake working a mathematical problem . . . going back to the point of error and going on again from there.

"Well, I'll be . . . " Mr. Meek said.

Meek stiffened and the stylus floated out of his hand, settled softly on the rock below.

A mathematical problem!

His breath gurgled in his throat.

He knew it now! He should have known it all the time. But the mechanic had talked about the bugs playing games and so had Hamilton. That had thrown him off.

Games! Those bugs weren't playing any game. They were solving mathematical equations!

Meek leaned forward to watch, forgetting where he was. One of the stilts slipped out of position and Meek felt himself starting to fall. He dropped the notebook and frantically clawed at empty space.

The other stilt went, then, and Meek found himself floating slowly downward, gravity weak but inexorable. His struggle to retain his balance had flung him forward, away from the face of the rock, and he was falling directly over the board on which the bugs were arrayed.

He pawed and kicked at space, but still floated down, course unchanged. He struck and bounced, struck and bounced again.

On the fourth bounce he managed to hook his fingers around a tiny projection of the surface. Fighting desperately, he regained his feet.

Something scurried across the face of his helmet and he lifted his hand before him. It was covered with the bugs.

Fumbling desperately, he snapped on the rocket motor of his suit, shot out into space, heading for the rock where the lights from the ports of Hamilton's shack blinked with the weaving of the rock.

Oliver Meek shut his eyes and groaned.

"Gus will give me hell for this," he told himself.

Gus shook the small wooden box thoughtfully, listening to the frantic scurrying within it.

"By rights," he declared, judiciously, "I should take this over and dump it in Bud's ship. Get even with him for swiping my injector."

"But you got the injector back," Meek pointed out.

"Oh, sure, I got it back," admitted Gus. "But it wasn't orthodox, it wasn't. Just getting your property back ain't getting even. I never did have a chance to smack Bud in the snoot the way I should of smacked him. Moe talked me into it. He was the one that had the idea the welfare lady should go over and talk to Bud. She must of laid it on thick, too, about how we should settle down and behave ourselves and all that. Otherwise Bud never would have given her that injector."

He shook his head dolefully. "This here Ring ain't ever going to be the same again. If we don't watch out, we'll find ourselves being polite to one another."

"That would be awful," agreed Meek.

"Wouldn't it, though," declared Gus.

Meek squinted his eyes and pounced on the follor, scrabbling on hands and knees after a scurrying thing that twinkled in the lamplight.

"Got him," yelped Meek, scooping the shining mote up in his hand.

Gus inched the lid off the wooden box top. Meek rose and popped the bug inside.

"That makes twenty-eight of them," said Meek.

"I told you," Gus accused him, "that we hadn't got them all. You better take another good look at your suit. The danged things burrow right into solid metal and pull the hole in after them, seems like. Sneakiest cusses in the whole dang system. Just like chiggers back on Earth."

"Chiggers," Meek told him, "burrow into a person to lay eggs."

"Maybe these things do, too," Gus contended.

The radio on the mantel blared a warning signal, automatically tuning in on one of the regular newscasts from Titan City out on Saturn's biggest moon.

The syrupy, chamber-of-commerce voice of the announcer was shaky with excitement and pride.

"Next week," he said, "the annual Martian-Earth football game will be played at Greater New York on Earth. But in the Earth's newspapers tonight another story has pushed even that famous classic of the sporting world down into secondary place."

He paused and took a deep breath and his voice practically yodeled with delight.

"The sporting event, ladies' and gentlemen, that is being

talked up and down the streets of Earth tonight, is one that will be played here in our own Saturnian system. A space-polo game. To be played by two unknown, pick-up, amateur teams down in the Inner Ring. Most of the men have never played polo before. Few, if any of them, have even seen a game. There may have been some of them who didn't, at first, know what it was.

"But they're going to play it. The men who ride those bucking rocks that make up the Inner Ring will go out into space in their rickety ships and fight it out. And, ladies and gentlemen, when I say fight it out, I really mean fight it out. For the game, it seems, will be a sort of tournament, the final battle in a feud that has been going on in the Ring for years. No one knows what started the feud. It has gotten so it really doesn't matter. The only thing that matters is that when men from Sector Twenty-Three meet those from Sector Thirty-Seven, the feud is taken up again. But that is at an end now. In a few days the feud will be played out to its bitter end when the ships from the Inner Ring go out into space to play that most dangerous of all sports, space polo. For the outcome of that game will decide, forever, the supremacy of one of the two sectors."

Meek rose from his chair, opened his mouth as if to speak, but sank back again when Gus hissed at him and held a finger to his lips for silence.

"The teams are now in training," went on the newscaster, the happy lilt in his voice still undimmed, "and it is understood that Sector Twenty-Three has the advantage, at the start, at least, of having a polo expert as its coach. Just who this expert is no one can say. Several names have been mentioned, but . . ."

"No, no," yelped Meek, struggling to his feet, but Gus shushed him, poking a finger toward him and grinning like a bearded imp.

". . . Bets are mounting high throughout the entire Saturnian system," the announcer was saying, "but since little is known about the teams, the odds still are even. It is likely, however, that odds will be demanded on the Sector Thirty-Seven team on the basis of the story about the expert coach.

"The very audacity of such a game has attracted solar-wide

attention and special fleets of ships will leave both Earth and Mars within the next few days to bring spectators to the game. Newsmen from the inner worlds, among them some of the system's most famous sports writers, are already on their way.

"Originally intended to be no more than a recreation project under the supervision of the Department of Health and Welfare, the game has suddenly become a solar attraction. The *Daily Rocket* back on Earth is offering a gigantic loving cup for the winning team, while the *Morning Spaceways* has provided another loving cup, only slightly smaller, to be presented the player adjudged the most valuable to his team. We may have more to tell you about the game before the newscast is over, but in the meantime we shall go on to other news of solar int——"

Meek leaped up. "He meant me," he whooped. "That was me he meant when he was talking about a famous coach!"

"Sure," said Gus. "He couldn't have meant anyone else but you."

"But I'm not a famous coach," protested Meek. "I'm not even a coach at all. I never saw but one space-polo game in all my life. I hardly know how it's played. I just know you go up there in space and bat a ball around. I'm going to——"

"You ain't going to do a blessed thing," said Gus. "You ain't skipping out on us. You're staying right here and give us all the fine pointers of the game. Maybe you ain't so hot as the newscaster made out, but you're a dang sight better than anyone else around here. At least you seen a game once and that's more than any of the rest of us have."

"But I——"

"I don't know what's the matter with you," declared Gus. "You're just pretending you don't know anything about polo, that's all. Maybe you're a fugitive from justice. Maybe that's why you're so anxious to make a getaway. Only reason you stopped at all was because your ship got stoved up."

"I'm no fugitive," declared Meek, drawing himself up. "I'm just a bookkeeper out to see the system."

"Forget it," said Gus. "Forget it. Nobody around here's going to give you away. If they even so much as peep, I'll plain paralyze them. So you're a bookkeeper. That's good enough for me. Just let anyone say you ain't a bookkeeper and see what happens to him.''

Meek opened his mouth to speak, closed it again. What was the use? Here he was, stuck again. Just like back on Juno when that preacher had thought he was a gunman and talked him into taking over the job of cleaning up the town. Only this time it was a space-polo game, and he knew even less about space polo than he did about being a lawman.

Gus rose and limped slowly across the room. Ponderously, he hauled a red bandanna out of his back pocket and carefully dusted off the one uncrowded space on the mantelshelf, between the alarm clock and the tarnished silver model of a rocket ship.

"Yes, sir," he said, "she'll look right pretty there."

He backed away and stared at the place on the shelf.

"I can almost see her now," he said. "Glinting in the lamplight. Something to keep me company. Something to look at when I get lonesome."

"What are you talking about?" demanded Meek.

"That there cup the radio was talking about," said Gus. "The one for the most valuable team member."

Meek stammered. "But . . . but . . ."

"I'm going to win her," Gus declared.

IV

Saturn Inn bulged. Every room was crowded, with half a dozen to the cubicle, sleeping in relays. Those who couldn't find anywhere else to sleep spread blankets in the narrow corridors or dozed off in chairs or slept on the barroom floor. A few of them got stepped on.

Titan City's Junior Chamber of Commerce had done what it could to help the situation out, but the notice had been short. A half dozen nearby rocks which had been hastily leveled off for parking space now were jammed with hundreds of space vehicles, ranging from the nifty two-man job owned by Billy Jones, sports editor of the *Daily Rocket*, to the huge excursion liners sent out by the three big transport companies. A few hastily erected shelters helped out to some extent, but none of these shelters had a bar and were mostly untenanted.

Moe, the bartender at the Inn, harried with too many customers, droopy with lack of sleep, saw Oliver Meek bobbing around in the crowd that surged against the bar, much after the manner of a cork caught in a raging whirlpool. He reached out a hand and dragged Meek against the bar.

"Can't you do something to stop it?"

Meek blinked at him. "Stop what?"

"This game," said Moe. "It's awful, Mr. Meek. Honestly. The crowd has got the fellers so worked up, it's apt to be mass murder."

"I know it," Meek agreed, "but you can't stop it now. The Junior Chamber of Commerce would take the hide off anyone who even said he would like to see it stopped. It's more publicity than Saturn has gotten since the first expeditions were lost here."

"I don't like it," declared Moe, stolidly.

"I don't like it either," Meek confessed. "Gus and those other fellows on his team think I'm an expert. I told them what I knew about space polo, but it wasn't much. Trouble is they think it's everything there is to know. They figure they're a cinch to win and they got their shirts bet on the game. If they lose, they'll more than likely space-walk me."

Fingers tapped Meek's shoulders and he twisted around. A red face loomed above him, a cigarette drooping from the corner of its lips.

"Hear you say you was coaching the Twenty-Three bunch?"

Meek gulped.

"Billy Jones, that's me," said the lips with the cigarette. "Best damn sportswriter ever pounded keys. Been trying to find out who you was. Nobody else knows. Treat you right."

"You must be wrong," said Meek.

"Never wrong," insisted Jones. "Nose for news. Smell it out. Like this. *Sniff. Sniff.*"

His nose crinkled in imitation of a bloodhound, but his face didn't change otherwise. The cigarette still dangled, pouring smoke into a watery left eye.

"Heard the guy call you Meek," said Jones. "Name sounds familiar. Something about Juno, wasn't it? Rounded up a bunch of crooks. Found a space monster of some sort."

Another hand gripped Meek by the shoulder and literally jerked him around.

"So you're the guy!" yelped the owner of the hand. "I been looking for you. I've a good notion to smack you in the puss."

"Now, Bud," yelled Moe, in mounting fear, "you leave him alone. He ain't done a thing."

Meek gaped at the angry face of the hulking man, who still had his shoulder in the grip of a monstrous paw.

Bud Craney! The ring-rat that had stolen Gus's injector! The captain of the Thirty-Seven team.

"If there was room," Craney grated, "I'd wipe up the floor with you. But since there ain't, I'm just plain going to hammer you down about halfway into it."

"But he ain't done nothing!" shrilled Moe.

"He's an outsider, ain't he?" demanded Craney. "What business he got coming in there and messing around with things?"

"I'm not messing around with things, Mr. Craney," Meek declared, trying to be dignified about it. But it was hard to be dignified with someone lifting one by the shoulder so one's toes just barely touched the floor.

"All that's the matter with you," insisted the dangling Meek, "is that you know Gus and his men will give you a whipping. They'd done it, anyhow. I haven't helped them much. I haven't helped them hardly at all."

Craney howled in rage. "Why . . . you . . . you . . . ."

And then Oliver Meek did one of those things no one ever expected him to do, least of all himself.

"I'll bet you my spaceship," he said, "against anything you got."

Astonished, Craney opened his hand and let him down on the floor.

"You'll what?" he roared.

"I'll bet you my spaceship," said Meek, the madness still upon him, "that Twenty-Three will beat you."

He rubbed it in. "I'll even give you odds."

Craney gasped and sputtered. "I don't want any odds," he yelped. "I'll take it even. My moss patch against your ship."

Someone was calling Meek's name in the crowd.

"Mr. Meek! Mr. Meek!"

"Here," said Meek.

"What about that story?" demanded Billy Jones, but Meek didn't hear him.

A man was tearing his way through the crowd. It was one of the men from Twenty-Three.

"Mr. Meek," he panted, "you got to come right away. It's Gus. He's all tangled up with rheumatiz!"

Gus stared up with anguished eyes at Meek.

"It sneaked up on me while I slept," he squeaked. "Laid off me for years until just now. Limped once in a while, of course, and got a few twinges now and then, but that was all. Never had me tied up like this since I left Earth. One of the reasons I never did go back to Earth. Space is good climate for rheumatiz. Cold but dry. No moisture to get into your bones."

Meek looked around at the huddled men, saw the worry that was etched upon their faces.

"Get a hot-water bottle," he told one of them.

"Hell," said Russ Jensen, a hulking-framed spaceman, "there ain't no such a thing as a hot-water bottle nearer than Titan City."

"An electric pad, then."

Jensen shook his head. "No pads, neither. Only thing we can do is pour whiskey down him and if we pour enough down him to cure the rheumatiz, we'll get him drunk and he won't be no more able to play in that game than he is right now."

Meek's weak eyes blinked behind his glasses, staring at Gus.

"We'll lose sure if Gus can't play," said Jensen, "and me with everything I got bet on our team."

Another man spoke up. "Meek could play in Gus's place."

"Nope, he couldn't," declared Jensen. "The rats from Thirty-Seven wouldn't stand for it."

"They couldn't do a thing about it," declared the other man. "Meek's been here six weeks today. That makes him a resident. Six Earth weeks, the law says. And all that time he's been in Sector Twenty-Three. They wouldn't have a leg to stand on. They might squawk but they couldn't make it stick."

"You're certain of that?" demanded Jensen.

"Dead certain," said the other.

Meek saw them looking at him, felt a queasy feeling steal into his stomach.

"I couldn't," he told them. "I couldn't do it. I . . . I . . . ."

"You go right ahead, Oliver," said Gus. "I wanted to play, of course. Sort of set my heart on that cup. Had the mantelpiece all dusted off for it. But if I can't play, there ain't another soul I'd rather have play in my place than you."

"But I don't know a thing about polo," protested Meek.

"You taught it to us, didn't you?" bellowed Jensen. "You pretended like you knew everything there was to know."

"But I didn't," insisted Meek. 'You wouldn't let me explain. You kept telling me all the time what a swell coach I was and when I tried to argue with you and tell you that I wasn't you yelled me down. I never saw more than one game in all my life and the only reason I saw it then was because I found the ticket. It was on the sidewalk and I picked it up. Somebody had dropped it."

"So you been stringing us along," yelped Jensen. "You been making fools of us! How do we know but you showed us wrong. You been giving us the wrong dope."

He advanced on Meek and Meek backed against the wall.

Jensen lifted his fist, held it in front of him as if he were weighing it.

"I ought to bop you one," he decided. "All of us had ought to bop you one. Every danged man in this here room has got his shirt bet on the game because we figured we couldn't lose with a coach like you."

"So have I," said Meek. But it wasn't until he said it that he really realized he did have his shirt bet on Twenty-Three. His spaceship. It wasn't all he had, of course, but it was the thing that was nearest to his heart . . . the thing he had slaved for thirty years to buy.

He suddenly remembered those years now. Years of bending over account books in the dingy office back on Earth, watching other men go out in space, longing to go himself. Counting pennies so that he could go. Spending only a dime for lunch and eating crackers and cheese instead of going out for dinner in the evening. Piling up the dollars, slowly through the years . . . dollars to buy the ship that now stood out on the field, all damage repaired. Sitting poised for space.

But if Thirty-Seven won, it wouldn't be his any longer. It would be Craney's. He'd just made a bet with Craney and there were plenty of witnesses to back it up.

"Well?" demanded Jensen.

"I will play," said Meek.

"And you really know about the game? You wasn't kidding us?"

Meek looked at the men before him and the expression on their faces shaped his answer.

He gulped . . . gulped again. Then slowly he nodded.

"Sure, I know about it," he lied.

They didn't look quite satisfied.

He glanced around, but there was no way of escape. He faced them again, back pressed against the wall.

He tried to make his voice light and breezy, but he couldn't quite keep out the croak.

"Haven't played it much in the last few years," he said, "but back when I was a kid I was a ten-goal man."

They were satisfied at that.

V

Hunched behind the controls, Meek slowly circled Gus's crate, waiting for the signal, half fearful of what would happen when it came.

Glancing to left and right, he could see the other ships of

Sector Twenty-Three, slowly circling too, red identification lights strung along their hulls.

Ten miles away a gigantic glowing ball danced in the middle of the space-field, bobbing around like a jigging lantern. And beyond it were the circling blue lights of the Thirty-Seven team. And beyond them the glowing green space-buoys that marked the Thirty-Seven goal line.

Meek bent an attentive ear to the ticking of the motor, listening intently for the alien click he had detected a moment before. Gus's ship, to tell the truth, was none too good. It might have been a good ship once, but now it was worn out. It was sluggish and slow to respond to the controls, it had a dozen little tricks that kept one on the jump. It had followed space trails too long, had plumped down to too many bumpy landings in the maelstrom of the Belt.

Meek sighed gustily. It would have been different if they had let him take his own ship, but it was only on the condition that he use Gus's ship that Thirty-Seven had agreed to let him play at all. They had raised a fuss about it, but Twenty-Three had the law squarely on its side.

He stole a glance toward the sidelines and saw hundreds of slowly cruising ships. Ships crammed with spectators out to watch the game. Radio ships that would beam a play-by-play description to be channeled to every radio station throughout the solar system. Newsreel ships that would film the clash of opposing craft. Ships filled with newsmen who would transmit reams of copy back to Earth and Mars.

Looking at them, Meek shuddered.

How in the world had he ever let himself get into a thing like this? He was out to see the solar system, not to play a polo game . . . especially a polo game he didn't want to play.

It had been the bugs, of course. If it hadn't been for the bugs, Gus never would have had the chance to talk him into that coaching business.

He should have spoken out, of course. Told them, flat out, that he didn't know a thing about polo. Made them understand he wasn't going to have a thing to do with this silly scheme. But they had shouted at him and laughed at him and bullied him.

Been nice to him, too. That was the biggest trouble. He was a sucker, he knew, for anyone who was nice to him. Not many people had been.

Maybe he should have gone to Miss Henrietta Perkins and explained. She might have listened and understood. Although he wasn't any too sure about that. She probably had plenty to do with starting the publicity rolling. After all, it was her job to make a showing in the jobs she did.

If it hadn't been for Gus's dusting off the place on the mantelpiece. If it hadn't been for the Titan City Junior Chamber of Commerce. If it hadn't been for all the ballyhoo about the mystery coach.

But more especially, if he'd kept his fool mouth shut and not made that bet with Craney.

Meek groaned and tried to remember the few things he did know about polo. And he couldn't think of a single thing, not even some of the things he had made up and told the boys.

Suddenly a rocket flared from the referee's ship and with a jerk Meek hauled back the throttle. The ship gurgled and stuttered and for a moment, heart in his throat, Meek thought it was going to blow up right then and there.

But it didn't. It gathered itself together and leaped, forcing Meek hard against the chair, snapping back his head. Dazed, he reached out for the repulsor trigger.

Ahead the glowing ball bounced and quivered, jumped this way and that as the ships spun in a mad melee with repulsor beams whipping out like stabbing knives.

Two of the ships crashed and fell apart like matchboxes. A third, trying a sharp turn above the field of play, came unstuck and strewed itself across fifty miles of space.

Substitute ships dashed in from the sidelines, signaled by the referee's blinking light. Rescue ships streaked out to pick up the players, salvage ships to clear away the pieces.

For a fleeting moment, Meek got the bobbing sphere in the cross-hairs and squeezed the trigger. The ball jumped as if someone had smacked it with his fist, sailed across the field.

Fighting to bring the ship around, Meek yelled in fury at its slowness. Desperately pouring on the juice, he watched with agony as a blue-lighted ship streamed down across the void, heading for the ball.

The ship groaned in every joint, protesting and twisting as if in agony, as Meek forced it around. Suddenly there was a snap and the sudden *swoosh* of escaping air. Startled, Meek looked up. Bare ribs stood out against star-spangled space. A plate had been ripped off!

Face strained behind the visor of his spacesuit, hunched over the controls, he waited for the rest of the plates to go. By some miracle they hung on. One worked loose and flapped weirdly as the ship shivered in the turn.

But the turn had taken too long and Meek was too late. The blue-lamped ship already had the ball, was streaking for the goal line. Jensen somehow had had sense enough to refuse to be sucked out of goalie position, and now he charged in to intercept.

But he muffed his chance. He dived in too fast and missed with his repulsor beam by a mile at least. The ball sailed over the lighted buoys and the first chukker was over, with Thirty-Seven leading by one score.

The ships lined up again.

The rocket flared from the starter's ship and the ships plunged out. One of Thirty-Seven's ships began to lose things. Plates broke loose and fell away, a rocket snapped its moorings and sailed off at a tangent, spouting gouts of flame, the structural ribs came off and strewed themselves along like spilling toothpicks.

Battered by repulsor beams, the ball suddenly bounced upward and Meek, trailing the field, waiting for just such a chance, played a savage tune on the tube controls.

The ship responded with a snap, executing a half-roll and a hairpin turn that shook the breath from Meek. Two more plates tore off in the turn, but the ship plowed on. Now the ball was dead ahead and Meek gave it the works. The beam hit squarely and Meek followed through. The second chukker was over and the score was tied.

Not until he was curving back above the Thirty-Seven goal line did Meek have time to wonder what had happened to the ship. It was sluggish no longer. It was full of zip. Almost like driving his own sleek craft. Almost as if the ship knew where he wanted it to go and went there.

A hint of motion on the instrument panel caught his eye and he bent close to see what it was. He stiffened. The panel seemed to be alive. Seemed to be crawling.

He bent closer and froze. It was crawling. There was no doubt of that. Crawling with rock bugs.

Breath whistling between his teeth, Meek ducked his head under the panel. Every wire, every control was oozing bugs!

For a moment he sat paralyzed by the thoughts that flickered through his brain.

Gus, he knew, would have his scalp for this. Because he was the one who had brought the bugs over to the rock where Gus lived and kept the ship. They'd thought, of course, they had caught all of them that were on his suit, but now it was clear they hadn't. Some of them must have gotten away and found the ship. They would have made straight for it, of course, because of the alloys that were in it. Why bother with a spacesuit or anything else when there was a ship around?

Only there were too many of them. There were thousands in the instrument panel and other thousands in the controls and he couldn't have brought back that many. Not if he'd hauled them back in pails.

What was it Gus had said about their burrowing into metal just like chiggers burrow into human flesh?

Chiggers attacked humans to lay their eggs. Maybe . . . maybe . . .

A battalion of the bugs trooped across the face of an indicator and Meek saw they were smaller than the ones he had seen back on Gus's rock.

There was no doubt about it. They were young bugs. Bugs that had just hatched out. Thousands of them . . . millions of them, maybe! And they wouldn't be in the instruments and controls alone, but all through the ship. They'd be in the motors and the firing mechanisms . . . all the places where the best alloys were used.

Meek wrung his hands, watching them play tag across the

panel. If they'd had to hatch, why couldn't they have waited. Just until the game was over, anyhow. That would have been all he'd asked. But they hadn't and here he was, with a couple of million bugs or so right smack in his lap.

The rocket flared again and the ships shot out.

Bitterness chewing at him, Meek flung the ship out savagely. What did it matter what happened now? Gus would take the hide off him, rheumatism or no rheumatism, as soon as he found out about the bugs.

For a wild moment, he hoped he would crack up. Maybe the ship would fall apart like some of the others had. Like the old one-hoss shay the poet had written about centuries ago. The ship had lost so many plates that even now it was like flying a space-going box kite.

Suddenly a ship loomed directly ahead, diving from the zenith. Meek, forgetting his half-formed hope of a crackup a second before, froze in terror, but his fingers acted by pure instinct, stabbing at keys, although, in the petrified second that seemed half an eternity, Meek knew the ships would crash before he even touched the keys. And even as he thought it, the ship ducked in a nerve-rending jerk and they were skimming past, hulls almost touching. Another jerk and more plates gone and there was the ball, directly ahead, with the repulsor beam already licking out.

Meek's jaw fell and a chill went through his body and he couldn't move a muscle. For he hadn't even touched the trigger and yet the repulsor beam was flaring out, driving the ball ahead of it while the ship twisted and squirmed its way through a mass of fighting craft.

Hands dangling limply at his sides, Meek gaped in terror and disbelief. He wasn't touching the controls, and yet the ship was like a thing bewitched. A split second later the ball was over the goal and the ship was curving back, repulsor beam snapped off.

"It's the bugs!" Meek whispered to himself, lips scarcely moving. "The bugs have taken over!"

The craft he was riding, he knew, was no longer just a ship, but a collection of rock bugs. Bugs that could work out mathematical equations. And now were playing polo!

For what was polo, anyhow, except a mathematical equation, a problem of using certain points of force at certain points in space to arrive at a predetermined end? Back on Gus's rock the bugs had worked as a unit to solve equations . . . and the new hatch in the ship was working as a unit, too, to solve another kind of problem . . . the problem of taking a certain ball to a certain point despite certain variables and random factors in the form of opposing spaceships.

Tentatively, half fearfully, Meek stabbed cautiously at a key which should have turned the ship. The ship didn't turn. Meek snatched his hand away as if the key had burned his finger.

Back on the line the ship wheeled into position of its own accord and a moment later was off again. Meek clung to his chair with shaking hands. There was, he knew, no use of even pretending he was trying to operate the ship. There was just one thing that he was glad of. No one could see him sitting there, doing nothing.

But the time would come . . . and soon . . . when he would have to do something. For he couldn't let the ship return to the Ring. To do that would be to infest the other ships parked there, spread the bugs throughout the solar system. And those bugs definitely were something the solar system could get along without.

The ship shuddered and twisted, weaving its way through the pack of players. More plates ripped loose. Glancing up, Meek could see the glory of Saturn through the gleaming ribs.

Then the ball was over the line and Meek's team mates were shrieking at him over the radio in his spacesuit . . . happy, glee-filled yells of triumph. He didn't answer. He was too busy ripping out the control wires. But it didn't help. Even while he was doing it the ship went on unhampered and piled up another score.

Apparently the bugs didn't need the controls to make the ship do what they wanted. More than likely they were in control of the firing mechanism at its very source. Maybe, and the thought curled the hair on Meek's neck, they were the firing mechanism. Maybe they had integrated themselves with the very structure of the entire mechanism of the ship. That would make the ship alive. A living chunk of machinery that paid no attention to the man who sat at the controls.

Meanwhile, the ship made another goal. . . .

There was a way to stop the bugs . . . only one way . . . but it was dangerous.

But probably not half as dangerous, Meek told himself, as Gus or the Junior Chamber of Commerce or the Thirty-Seven team . . . especially the Thirty-Seven team . . . if any of them found out what was going on.

He found a wrench and crawled back along the shivering ship.

Working in a frenzy of fear and need for haste, Meek took off the plate that sealed the housing of the rear rocket assembly. Breath hissing in his throat, he fought the burrs that anchored the tubes. There were a lot of them and they didn't come off easily. Rockets had to be anchored securely . . . securely enough so the blast of atomic fire within their chambers wouldn't rip them free.

Meanwhile, the ship piled up the score.

Loose burrs rolled and danced along the floor and Meek knew the ship was in the thick of play again. Then they were curving back. Another goal!

Suddenly the rocket assembly shook a little, began to vibrate. Wielding the wrench like a madman, knowing he had seconds at the most, Meek spun two or three more bolts, then dropped the wrench and ran. Leaping for a hole from which a plate had been torn, he caught a rib, swung with every ounce of power he had, launching himself into space.

His right hand fumbled for the switch of the suit's rocket motor, found it, snapped it on to full acceleration. Something seemed to hit him on the head and he sailed into the depths of blackness.

VI

Billy Jones sat in the office of the repair shop, cigarette dangling from his lip, pouring smoke into his watery eye.

"Never saw anything like it in my life," he declared. "How

he made that ship go at all with half the plates ripped off is way beyond me."

The dungareed mechanic sighted along the toes of his shoes, planted comfortably on the desk.

"Let me tell you, mister," he declared, "the solar system never has known a pilot like him . . . never will again. He brought his ship down here with the instruments knocked out. Dead reckoning."

"Wrote a great piece about him," Billy said. "How he died in the best tradition of space. Stuff like that. The readers will eat it up. The way that ship let go he didn't have a chance. Seemed to go out of control all at once and went heaving and bucking almost into Saturn. Then, blooey . . . That's the end of it. One big splash of flame."

The mechanic squinted carefully at his toes. "They're still out there, messing around," he said, "but they'll never find him. When that ship blew up he was scattered halfway out to Pluto."

The inner lock swung open ponderously and a spacesuited figure stepped in.

They waited while he snapped back his helmet.

"Good evening, gentlemen," said Oliver Meek.

They stared, slack-jawed.

Jones was the first to recover. "But it can't be you! Your ship . . . it exploded!"

"I know," said Meek. "I got out just before it went. Turned on my suit rocket full blast. Knocked me out. By the time I came to I was halfway out to the second Ring. Took me a while to get back."

He turned to the mechanic. "Maybe you have a secondhand suit you would sell me. I have to get rid of this one. Has some bugs in it."

"Bugs? Oh, yes, I see. You mean something's wrong with it."

"That's it," said Meek. "Something's wrong with it."

"I got one I'll let you have, free for nothing," said the mechanic. "Boy, that was a swell game you played!"

"Could I have the suit now?" asked Meek. "I'm in a hurry to get away."

Jones bounced to his feet. "But you can't leave. Why, they think you're dead. They're out looking for you. And you won the cup . . . the cup as the most valuable team member."

"I just can't stay," said Meek. He shuffled his feet uneasily. "Got places to go. Things to see. Stayed too long already."

"But the cup . . ."

"Tell Gus I won the cup for him. Tell him to put it on that mantelpiece. In the place he dusted off for it."

"Meek's blue eyes shone queerly behind his glasses. "Tell him maybe he'll think of me sometimes when he looks at it."

The mechanic brought the suit. Meek bundled it under his arm, started for the lock.

Then turned back.

"Maybe you gentlemen . . ."

"Yes," said Jones.

"Maybe you can tell me how many goals I made. I lost count, you see."

"You made nine," said Jones.

Meek shook his head. "Must be getting old," he said. "When I was a kid I was a *ten-goal* man."

Then he was gone, the lock swinging shut behind him.

ARTHUR C. CLARK

Arthur C. Clarke is as famed for his pioneering nonfiction books about space travel (*Interplanetary Flight* appeared in 1950) as for his many fine science-fiction novels and stories. Here, in a wonder-filled adventure about the sailing ships of space, he combines his expert knowledge of the subject with his ability to make you feel as if *you* were in the cabin of his "sunjammer" along with John Merton. It's an experience you'll long remember.

Sunjammer

The enormous disk of sail strained at its rigging, already filled with the wind that blew between the worlds. In three minutes the race would begin, yet now John Merton felt more relaxed, more at peace, than at any time for the past year. Whatever happened when the Commodore gave the starting signal, whether *Diana* carried him to victory or defeat, he had achieved his ambition. After a lifetime spent in designing ships for others, now he would sail his own.

"*T* minus two minutes," said the cabin radio. "Please confirm your readiness."

One by one, the other skippers answered. Merton recognized all the voices—some tense, some calm—for they were the voices of his friends and rivals. On the four inhabited worlds, there were scarcely twenty men who could sail a sun-yacht; and they were all here, on the starting line or aboard the escort vessels, orbiting twenty-two thousand miles above the equator.

"Number One, *Gossamer*—ready to go."

"Number Two, *Santa Maria*—all O.K."

"Number Three, *Sunbeam*—O.K."

"Number Four, *Woomera*—all systems go."

Merton smiled at that last echo from the early, primitive days of astronautics. But it had become part of the tradition of space; and there were times when a man needed to evoke the shades of those who had gone before him to the stars.

"Number Five, *Lebedev*—we're ready."

"Number Six, *Arachne*—O.K."

Now it was his turn, at the end of the line; strange to think that the words he was speaking in this tiny cabin were being heard by at least five billion people.

"Number Seven, *Diana*—ready to start."

"One through Seven acknowledged." The voice from the judge's launch was impersonal. "Now T minus one minute."

Merton scarcely heard it; for the last time, he was checking the tension in the rigging. The needles of all the dynamometers were steady; the immense sail was taut, its mirror surface sparkling and glittering gloriously in the sun.

To Merton, floating weightless at the periscope, it seemed to fill the sky. As well it might—for out there were fifty million square feet of sail, linked to his capsule by almost a hundred miles of rigging. All the canvas of all the tea-clippers that had once raced like clouds across the China seas, sewn into one gigantic sheet, could not match the single sail that *Diana* had spread beneath the sun. Yet it was little more substantial than a soap bubble; that two square miles of aluminized plastic was only a few millionths of an inch thick.

"T minus ten seconds. All recording cameras on."

Something so huge, yet so frail, was hard for the mind to grasp. And it was harder still to realize that this fragile mirror could tow them free of Earth, merely by the power of the sunlight it would trap.

". . . Five, four, three, two, one, *cut!*"

Seven knife blades sliced through the seven thin lines tethering the yachts to the motherships that had assembled and serviced them.

Until this moment, all had been circling Earth together in a rigidly held formation, but now the yachts would begin to disperse, like dandelion seeds drifting before the breeze. And the winner would be the one who first drifted past the Moon.

Aboard *Diana*, nothing seemed to be happening. But Merton knew better; though his body could feel no thrust, the instrument board told him he was now accelerating at almost one thousandth of a gravity. For a rocket, that figure would have been ludicrous—but this was the first time any solar yacht had attained it. *Diana*'s design was sound; the vast sail was living up to his calculations. At this rate, two circuits of the Earth would built up his speed to escape velocity—then he could head out for the Moon, with the full force of the Sun behind him.

The full force of the Sun. He smiled wryly, remembering all his attempts to explain solar sailing to those lecture audiences back on Earth. That had been the only way he could raise money, in those early days. He might be Chief Designer of Cosmodyne Corporation, with a whole string of successful spaceships to his credit, but his firm had not been exactly enthusiastic about his hobby.

"Hold your hands out to the Sun," he'd said. "What do you feel? Heat, of course. But there's pressure as well—though you've never noticed it, because it's so tiny. Over the area of your hands, it only comes to about a millionth of an ounce.

"But out in space, even a pressure as small as that can be important—for it's acting all the time, hour after hour, day after day. Unlike rocket fuel, it's free and unlimited. If we want to, we can use it; we can build sails to catch the radiation blowing from the Sun."

At that point, he would pull out a few square yards of sail material and toss it towards the audience. The silvery film would coil and twist like smoke, then drift slowly to the ceiling in the hot-air currents.

"You can see how light it is," he'd continue. "A square mile weighs only a ton, and can collect five pounds of radiation pressure. So it will start moving—and we can let it tow us along, if we attach rigging to it.

"Of course, its acceleration will be tiny—about a thousandth of a g. That doesn't seem much, but let's see what it means.

"It means that in the first second, we'll move about a fifth of an inch. I suppose a healthy snail could do better than that. But after a minute, we've covered sixty feet, and will be doing just over a mile an hour. That's not bad, for something driven by pure sunlight! After an hour, we're forty miles from our starting point, and will be moving at eighty miles an hour. Please remember that in space there's no friction, so once you start anything moving, it will keep going forever. You'll be surprised when I tell you what our thousandth-of-a-g sailing boat will be doing at the end of a day's run. *Almost two thousand miles an hour!* If it starts from orbit—as it has to, of course—it can reach escape velocity in a couple of days. And all without burning a single drop of fuel!''

Well, he'd convinced them, and in the end he'd even convinced Cosmodyne. Over the last twenty years, a new sport had come into being. It had been called the sport of billionaires, and that was true—but it was beginning to pay for itself in terms of publicity and television coverage. The prestige of four continents and two worlds was riding on this race, and it had the biggest audience in history.

Diana had made a good start; time to take a look at the opposition. Moving very gently. Though there were shock absorbers between the control capsule and the delicate rigging, he was determined to run no risks. Merton stationed himself at the periscope.

There they were, looking like strange silver flowers planted in the dark fields of space. The nearest, South America's *Santa Maria*, was only fifty miles away; it bore a resemblance to a boy's kite—but a kite more than a mile on its side. Farther away, the University of Astrograd's *Lebedev* looked like a Maltese cross; the sails that formed the four arms could apparently be tilted for steering purposes. In contrast, the Federation of Australasia's *Woomera* was a simple parachute, four miles in circumference. General Spacecraft's *Arachne*, as its name suggested, looked like a spider web—and had been built on the same principles, by robot shuttles spiraling out from a central point. Eurospace Corporation's *Gossamer* was an identical design, on a slightly smaller scale. And the Republic of Mars's *sunbeam* was a flat ring, with a half-mile-wide hole in the center, spinning slowly so that centrifugal force gave it stiffness. That was an old idea, but no one had ever made it work. Merton was fairly sure that the colonials would be in trouble when they started to turn.

That would not be for another six hours, when the yachts had moved along the first quarter of their slow and stately twenty-four hour orbit. Here at the beginning of the race, they were all heading directly away from the Sun—running, as it were, before the solar wind. One had to make the most of this lap, before the boats swung around to the other side of Earth and then started to head back into the Sun.

Time for the first check, Merton told himself, while he had no navigational worries. With the periscope, he made a careful examination of the sail, concentrating on the points where the rigging was attached to it. The shroud lines—narrow bands of unsilvered plastic film—would have been completely invisible had they not been coated with fluorescent paint. Now they were taut lines of colored light, dwindling away for hundreds of yards towards that gigantic sail. Each had its own electric windlass, not much bigger than a game fisherman's reel. The little windlasses were continually turning, playing lines in or out, as the autopilot kept the sail trimmed at the correct angle to the Sun.

The play of sunlight on the great flexible mirror was beautiful to watch. It was undulating in slow, stately oscillations, sending multiple images of the Sun marching across the heavens, until they faded away at the edges of the sail. Such leisurely vibrations were to be expected in this vast and flimsy structure; they were usually quite harmless, but Merton watched them carefully. Sometimes they could build up to the catastrophic undulations known as the wriggles, which could tear a sail to pieces.

When he was satisfied that everything was shipshape, he swept the periscope around the sky, rechecking the positions of his rivals. It was as he had hoped; the weeding-out process had begun, as the less efficient boats fell astern. But the real test would come when they passed into the shadow of the Earth; then maneuverability would count as much as speed.

It seemed a strange thing to do, now that the race had just started, but it might be a good idea to get some sleep. The two-man crews on the other boats could take it in turns, but Merton had no one to relieve him. He must rely on his physical resources—like that other solitary seaman Joshua Slocum, in his tiny *Spray*. The American skipper had sailed *Spray* single-handed around the world; he could never have dreamed that, two centuries later, a man would be sailing single-handed from Earth to Moon—inspired, at least partly, by his example.

Merton snapped the elastic bands of the cabin seat around his waist and legs, then placed the electrodes of the sleep-inducer on his forehead. He set the timer for three hours, and relaxed.

Very gently, hypnotically, the electronic pulses throbbed in the frontal lobes of his brain. Colored spirals of light expanded beneath his closed eyelids, widening outwards to infinity. Then—nothing. . . .

The brazen clamor of the alarm dragged him back from his dreamless sleep. He was instantly awake, his eyes scanning the instrument panel. Only two hours had passed—but above the accelerometer a red light was flashing. Thrust was falling; *Diana* was losing power.

Merton's first thought was that something had happened to the sail; perhaps the antispin devices had failed, and the rigging had become twisted. Swiftly, he checked the meters that showed the tension in the shroud lines. Strange, on one side of the sail they were reading normally—but on the other the pull was dropping slowly even as he watched.

In sudden understanding, Merton grabbed the periscope, switched to wide-angle vision, and started to scan the edge of the sail. Yes—there was the trouble, and it could have only one cause.

A huge, sharp-edged shadow had begun to slide across the gleaming silver of the sail. Darkness was falling upon *Diana*, as if a cloud had passed between her and the Sun. And in the dark, robbed of the rays that drove her, she would lose all thrust and drift helplessly through space.

But, of course, there were no clouds here, more than twenty thousand miles above Earth. If there was a shadow, it must be made by man.

Merton grinned as he swung the periscope towards the Sun, switching in the filters that would allow him to look full into its blazing face without being blinded.

"Maneuver Four *a*," he muttered to himself. "We'll see who can play best at *that* game."

It looked as if a giant planet were crossing the face of the Sun. A great black disk had bitten deep into its edge. Twenty miles astern, *Gossamer* was trying to arrange an artificial eclipse—specially for *Diana*'s benefit.

The maneuver was a perfectly legitimate one; back in the days of ocean racing, skippers had often tried to rob each other of the wind. With any luck, you could leave your rival becalmed, with his sails collapsing around him—and be well ahead before he could undo the damage.

Merton had no intention of being caught so easily. There was plenty of time to take evasive action; things happened very slowly when you were running a solar sailing boat. It would be at least twenty minutes before *Gossamer* could slide completely across the face of the Sun, and leave him in darkness.

Diana's tiny computer—the size of a matchbox, but the equivalent of a thousand human mathematicians—considered the problem for a full second and then flashed the answer. He'd have to open control panels three and four, until the sail had developed an extra twenty degrees of tilt; then the radiation pressure would blow him out of *Gossamer*'s dangerous shadow, back into the full blast of the Sun. It was a pity to interfere with the autopilot, which had been carefully programmed to give the fastest possible run—but that, after all, was why he was here. This was what made solar yachting a sport, rather than a battle between computers.

Out went control lines one to six, slowly undulating like sleepy snakes as they momentarily lost their tension. Two miles away, the triangular panels began to open lazily, spilling sunlight through the sail. Yet, for a long time, nothing seemed to happen. It was hard to grow accustomed to this slow-motion world, where it took minutes for the effects of any action to become visible to the eye. Then Merton saw that the sail was indeed tipping towards the Sun—and that *Gossamer*'s shadow was sliding harmlessly away, its cone of darkness lost in the deeper night of space.

Long before the shadow had vanished and the disk of the Sun had cleared again, he reversed the tilt and brought *Diana* back on course. Her new momentum would carry her clear of the danger; no need to overdo it, and upset his calculations by sidestepping too far. That was another rule that was hard to learn. The very moment you had started something happening in space, it was already time to think about stopping it.

He reset the alarm, ready for the next natural or man-made emergency; perhaps *Gossamer*, or one of the other contestants, would try the same trick again. Meanwhile, it was time to eat, though he did not feel particularly hungry. One used little physical energy in space, and it was easy to forget about food. Easy—and dangerous; for when an emergency arose; you might not have the reserves needed to deal with it.

He broke open the first of the meal packets and inspected it without enthusiasm. The name on the label—SPACETASTIES—was enough to put him off. And he had grave doubts about the promise printed underneath. "Guaranteed crumbless." It had been said that crumbs were a greater danger to space vehicles than meteorites. They could drift into the most unlikely places, causing short circuits, blocking vital jets and getting into instruments that were supposed to be hermetically sealed.

Still, the liverwurst went down pleasantly enough; so did the chocolate and the pineapple puree. The plastic coffee-bulb was warming on the electric heater when the outside world broke in on his solitude. The radio operator on the Commodore's launch routed a call to him.

"Dr. Merton? If you can spare the time, Jeremy Blair would like a few words with you." Blair was one of the more responsible news commentators, and Merton had been on his program many times. He could refuse to be interviewed, of course, but he liked Blair, and at the moment he could certainly not claim to be too busy. "I'll take it," he answered.

"Hello, Dr. Merton," said the commentator immediately. "Glad you can spare a few minutes. And congratulations—you seem to be ahead of the field."

"Too early in the game to be sure of that," Merton answered cautiously.

"Tell me, Doctor—why did you decide to sail *Diana* yourself? Just because it's never been done before?"

"Well, isn't that a very good reason? But it wasn't the only one, of course." He paused, choosing his words carefully. "You know how critically the performance of a sun-yacht depends on its mass. A second man, with all his supplies, would mean another five hundred pounds. That could easily be the difference between winning and losing."

"And you're quite certain that you can handle *Diana* alone?"

"Reasonably sure, thanks to the automatic controls I've designed. My main job is to supervise and make decisions."

"But—two square miles of sail! It just doesn't seem possible for one man to cope with all that!"

Merton laughed.

"Why not? Those two square miles produce a maximum pull of just ten pounds. I can exert more force with my little finger."

"Well, thank you, Doctor. And good luck."

As the commentator signed off, Merton felt a little ashamed of himself. For his answer had been only part of the truth; and he was sure that Blair was shrewd enough to know it.

There was just one reason why he was here, alone in space. For almost forty years he had worked with teams of hundreds or even thousands of men, helping to design the most complex vehicles that the world had ever seen. For the last twenty years he had led one of those teams, and watched his creations go soaring to the stars. (But there were failures that he could never forget, even though the fault had not been his.) He was famous, with a successful career behind him. Yet he had never done anything by himself; always he had been one of an army.

This was his very last chance of individual achievement, and he would share it with no one. There would be no more solar yachting for at least five years, as the period of the quiet Sun ended and the cycle of bad weather began, with radiation storms bursting through the solar system. When it was safe again for these frail, unshielded craft to venture aloft, he would be too old. If, indeed, he was not too old already. . . .

He dropped the empty food containers into the waste disposal, and turned once more to the periscope. At first, he could find only five of the other yachts; there was no sign of *Woomera*.

It took him several minutes to locate her—a dim, star-eclipsing phantom, neatly caught in the shadow of *Lebedev*. He could imagine the frantic efforts the Australasians were making to extricate themselves, and wondered how they had fallen into the trap. It suggested that *Lebedev* was unusually maneuverable; she would bear watching, though she was too far away to menace *Diana* at the moment.

Now the Earth had almost vanished. It had waned to a narrow, brilliant bow of light that was moving steadily towards the Sun. Dimly outlined within that burning bow was the night side of the planet, with the phosphorescent gleams of great cities showing here and there through gaps in the clouds. The disk of darkness had already blanked out a huge section of the Milky Way; in a few minutes, it would start to encroach upon the Sun.

The light was fading. A purple, twilight hue—the glow of many sunsets, thousands of miles below—was falling across the sail, as *Diana* slipped silently into the shadow of Earth. The Sun plummeted below that invisible horizon. Within minutes, it was night.

Merton looked back along the orbit he had traced now a quarter of the way around the world. One by one he saw the brilliant stars of the other yachts wink out, as they joined him in the brief night. It would be an hour before the Sun emerged from that enormous black shield, and through all that time they would be completely helpless, coasting without power.

He switched on the external spotlight, and started to search the now darkened sail with its beam. Already, the thousands of acres of film were beginning to wrinkle and become flaccid; the shroud lines were slackening and must be wound in lest they become entangled. But all this was expected; everything was going as planned.

Forty miles astern, *Arachne* and *Santa Maria* were not so lucky. Merton learned of their troubles when the radio burst into life on the emergency circuit.

"Number Two, Number Six—this is Control. You are on a collision course. Your orbits will intersect in sixty-five minutes! Do you require assistance?"

There was a long pause while the two skippers digested this bad news. Merton wondered who was to blame; perhaps one yacht had been trying to shadow the other, and had not completed the maneuver before they were both caught in darkness. Now there was nothing that either could do; they were slowly but inexorably converging together, unable to change course by a fraction of a degree.

Yet, sixty-five minutes! That would just bring them out into sunlight again, as they emerged from the shadow of the Earth. They still had a slim chance, if their sails could snatch enough power to avoid a crash. There must be some frantic calculations going on aboard *Arachne* and *Santa Maria*.

Arachne answered first; her reply was just what Merton had expected.

"Number Six calling Control. We don't need assistance, thank you. We'll work this out for ourselves."

I wonder, thought Merton. But at least it will be interesting to watch. The first real drama of the race was approaching—exactly above the line of midnight on the sleeping Earth.

For the next hour, Merton's own sail kept him too busy to worry about *Arachne* and *Santa Maria*. It was hard to keep a good watch on that fifty million square feet of dim plastic out there in the darkness, illuminated only by his narrow spotlight and the rays of the still-distant Moon. From now on, for almost half his orbit around the Earth, he must keep the whole of this immense area edge-on to the Sun. During the next twelve or fourteen hours, the sail would be a useless encumbrance; for he would be heading into the Sun, and its rays could only drive him backwards along his orbit. It was a pity that he could not furl the sail completely, until he was ready to use it again. But no one had yet found a practical way of doing this.

Far below, there was the first hint of dawn along the edge of the Earth. In ten minutes, the Sun would emerge from its eclipse; the coasting yachts would come to life again as the blast of radiation struck their sails. That would be the moment of crisis for *Arachne* and *Santa Maria*—and, indeed, for all of them.

Merton swung the periscope until he found the two dark shadows drifting against the stars. They were very close together—perhaps less than three miles apart. They might, he decided, just be able to make it. . . .

Dawn flashed like an explosion along the rim of Earth, as the Sun rose out of the Pacific. The sail and shroud lines glowed a brief crimson, then gold, then blazed with the pure white light of day. The needles of the dynamometers began to lift from their zeros—but only just. *Diana* was still almost completely weightless, for with the sail pointing towards the Sun, her acceleration was now only a few millionths of a gravity.

But *Arachne* and *Santa Maria* were crowding on all the sail they could manage, in their desperate attempt to keep apart. Now, while there was less than two miles between them, their glittering plastic clouds were unfurling and expanding with agonizing slowness, as they felt the first delicate push of the Sun's rays. Almost every TV screen on Earth would be mirroring this protracted drama; and even now, at this very last minute, it was impossible to tell what the outcome would be.

The two skippers were stubborn men. Either could have cut his sail, and fallen back to give the other a chance; but neither would do so. Too much prestige, too many millions, too many reputations were at stake. And so, silently and softly as snowflakes falling on a winter night, *Arachne* and *Santa Maria* collided.

The square kite crawled almost imperceptibly into the circular spider's-web; the long ribbons of the shroud lines twisted and tangled together with dreamlike slowness. Even aboard *Diana*, busy with his own rigging, Merton could scarcely tear his eyes away from this silent, long-drawn-out disaster.

For more than ten minutes the billowing, shining clouds continued to merge into one inextricable mass. Then the crew capsules tore loose and went their separate ways, missing each other by hundreds of yards. With a flare of rockets, the safety launches hurried to pick them up.

That leaves five of us, thought Merton. He felt sorry for the skippers who had so thoroughly eliminated each other, only a few hours after the start of the race; but they were young men, and would have another chance.

Within minutes, the five had dropped to four. From the very beginning, Merton had had doubts about the slowly rotating *Sunbeam*. Now he saw them justified.

The Martian ship had failed to tack properly; her spin had given her too much stability. Her great ring of a sail was turning to face the Sun, instead of being edge-on to it. She was being blown back along her course at almost her maximum acceleration.

That was about the most maddening thing that could happen to a skipper—worse even than a collision, for he could blame only himself. But no one would feel much sympathy for the frustrated colonials, as they dwindled slowly astern. They had made too many brash boasts before the race, and what had happened to them was poetic justice.

Yet it would not do to write off *Sunbeam* completely. With almost half a million miles still to go, she might still pull ahead. Indeed, if there were a few more casualties, she might be the only one to complete the race. It had happened before.

However, the next twelve hours were uneventful, as the Earth waxed in the sky from new to full. There was little to do while the fleet drifted around the unpowered half of its orbit, but Merton did not find the time hanging heavily on his hands. He caught a few hours' sleep, ate two meals, wrote up his log, and became involved in several more radio interviews. Sometimes, though rarely, he talked to the other skippers, exchanging greetings and friendly taunts. But most of the time he was content to float in weightless relaxation, beyond all the cares of Earth, happier than he had been for many years. He was—as far as any man could be in space—master of his own fate, sailing the ship upon which he had lavished so much skill, so much love that she had become part of his very being.

The next casualty came when they were passing the line between Earth and Sun, and were just beginning the powered half of the orbit. Aboard *Diana*, Merton saw the great sail stiffen as it tilted to catch the rays that drove it. The acceleration began to climb up from the microgravities, though it would be hours yet before it would reach its maximum value.

It would never reach it for *Gossamer*. The moment when power came on again was always critical, and she failed to survive it.

Blair's radio commentary, which Merton had left running at low volume, alerted him with the news: "Hello, *Gossamer* has the wriggles!" He hurried to the periscope, but at first could see nothing wrong with the great circular disk of *Gossamer*'s sail. It was difficult to study it, as it was almost edge-on to him and so appeared as a thin ellipse; but presently he saw that it was twisting back and forth in slow, irresistible oscillations. Unless the crew could damp out these waves, by properly timed but gentle tugs on the shroud lines, the sail would tear itself to pieces.

They did their best, and after twenty minutes it seemed that they had succeeded. Then, somewhere near the center of the sail, the plastic film began to rip. It was slowly driven outwards by the radiation pressure, like smoke coiling upwards from a fire. Within a quarter of an hour, nothing was left but the delicate tracery of the radial spars that had supported the great web. Once again there was a flare of rockets as a launch moved in to retrieve the *Gossamer*'s capsule and her dejected crew.

"Getting rather lonely up here, isn't it?" said a conversational voice over the ship-to-ship radio.

"Not for you, Dimitri," retorted Merton. "You've still got company back there at the end of the field. I'm the one who's lonely, up here in front." It was not an idle boast. By this time *Diana* was three hundred miles ahead of the next competitor, and Merton's lead should increase still more rapidly in the hours to come.

Aboard *Lebedev*, Dimitri Markoff gave a good-natured chuckle. He did not sound, Merton thought, at all like a man who had resigned himself to defeat.

"Remember the legend of the tortoise and the hare," answered the Russian. "A lot can happen in the next quarter-million miles."

It happened much sooner than that, when they had completed their first orbit of Earth and were passing the starting line again—though thousands of miles higher, thanks to the extra energy the Sun's rays had given them. Merton had taken careful sights on the other yachts, and had fed the figures into the computer. The answer it gave for Woomera was so absurd that he immediately did a recheck.

There was no doubt of it—the Australasians were catching up at a fantastic rate. No solar yacht could possibly have such an acceleration, unless—

A swift look through the periscope gave the answer. Woomera's rigging, pared back to the very minimum of mass, had given way. It was her sail alone, still maintaining its shape, that was racing up behind him like a handkerchief blown before the wind. Two hours later it fluttered past, less than twenty miles away. But long before that, the Australasians had joined the growing crowd aboard the Commodore's launch.

So now it was a straight fight between Dianna and Lebedev—for though the Martians had not given up, they were a thousand miles astern and no longer counted as a serious threat. For that matter, it was hard to see what Lebedev could do to overtake Diana's lead. But all the way around the second lap —through eclipse again, and the long, slow drift against the Sun, Merton felt a growing unease.

He knew the Russian pilots and designers. They had been trying to win this race for twenty years and after all, it was only fair that they should, for had not Pyotr Nikolayevich Lebedev been the first man to detect the pressure of sunlight, back at the very beginning of the twentieth century? But they had never succeeded.

And they would never stop trying. Dimitri was up to something—and it would be spectacular.

Aboard the official launch, a thousand miles behind the racing yachts, Commodore van Stratten looked at the radiogram with angry dismay. It had traveled more than a hundred million miles, from the chain of solar observatories swinging high above the blazing surface of the Sun, and it brought the worst possible news.

The Commodore—his title, of course, was purely honorary—back on Earth he was Professor of Astrophysics at Harvard—had been half expecting it. Never before had the race been arranged so late in the season; there had been many delays, they had gambled and now, it seemed, they might all lose.

Deep beneath the surface of the Sun, enormous forces were gathering. At any moment, the energies of a million hydrogen bombs might burst forth in the awesome explosion known as a solar flare. Climbing at millions of miles an hour, an invisible fireball many times the size of Earth would leap from the Sun, and head out across space.

The cloud of electrified gas would probably miss the Earth completely. But if it did not, it would arrive in just over a day. Spaceships could protect themselves, with their shielding and their powerful magnetic screen. But the lightly built solar yachts, with their paper-thin walls, were defenseless against such a menace. The crews would have to be taken off, and the race abandoned.

John Merton still knew nothing of this as he brought Diana around the Earth for the second time. If all went well, this would be the last circuit, both for him and for the Russians. They had spiraled upwards by thousands of miles, gaining energy from the Sun's rays. On this lap, they should escape from Earth completely—and head outwards on the long run to the Moon. It was a straight race now. Sunbeam's crew had finally withdrawn, exhausted, after battling valiantly with their spinning sail for more than a hundred thousand miles.

Merton did not feel tired; he had eaten and slept well, and Diana was behaving herself admirably. The autopilot, tensioning the rigging like a busy little spider, kept the great sail trimmed to the Sun more accurately than any human skipper —though, by this time, the two square miles of plastic sheet must have been riddled by hundreds of micrometeorites, the pinhead-sized punctures had produced no falling off of thrust.

He had only two worries. The first was shroud line number eight, which could no longer be adjusted properly. Without any warning, the reel had jammed; even after all these years of astronautical engineering, bearings sometimes seized up in vacuum. He could neither lengthen nor shorten the line, and would have to navigate as best he could with the others. Luckily, the most difficult maneuvers were over. From now on, Diana

would have the Sun behind her as she sailed straight down the
solar wind. And as the old-time sailors often said, it was easy to
handle a boat when the wind was blowing over your shoulder.

His other worry was *Lebedev*, still dogging his heels three
hundred miles astern. The Russian yacht had shown remarkable
maneuverability, thanks to the four great panels that could be
tilted around the central sail. All her flip-overs as she rounded
Earth had been carried out with superb precision; but to gain
maneuverability she must have sacrificed speed. You could not
have it both ways. In the long, straight haul ahead, Merton
should be able to hold his own. Yet he could not be certain of
victory until, three or four days from now, *Diana* went flashing
past the far side of the Moon.

And then, in the fiftieth hour of the race, near the end of the
second orbit around Earth, Markoff sprang his little surprise.

"Hello, John," he said casually, over the ship-to-ship circuit. "I'd like to watch this. It should be interesting."

Merton drew himself across to the periscope and turned up
the magnification to the limit. There in the field of view, a most
improbable sight against the background of the stars, was the
glittering Maltese cross of *Lebedev*, very small but very clear.
And then, as he watched, the four arms of the cross slowly
detached themselves from the central square and went drifting
away, with all their spars and rigging, into space.

Markoff had jettisoned all unnecessary mass, now that he
was coming up to escape velocity and need no longer plod
patiently around the Earth, gaining momentum on each circuit.
From now on, *Lebedev* would be almost unsteerable—but that
did not matter. All the tricky navigation lay behind her. It was as
if an old-time yachtsman had deliberately thrown away his
rudder and heavy keel—knowing that the rest of the race would
be straight downwind over a calm sea.

"Congratulations, Dimitri," Merton radioed. "It's a neat
trick. But it's not good enough—you can't catch up now."

"I've not finished yet," the Russian answered. "There's an
old winter's tale in my country, about a sleigh being chased by
wolves. To save himself, the driver has to throw off the passen-
gers one by one. Did you see the analogy?"

Merton did, all too well. On this final straight lap, Dimitri no longer needed his co-pilot. *Lebedev* could really be stripped down for action.

"Alexis won't be very happy about this," Merton replied. "Besides, it's against the rules."

"Alexis isn't happy, but I'm the captain. He'll just have to wait around for ten minutes until the Commodore picks him up. And the regulations say nothing about the size of the crew—you should know that."

Merton did not answer. He was too busy doing some hurried calculations, based on what he knew of *Lebedev*'s design. By the time he had finished, he knew that the race was still in doubt. *Lebedev* would be catching up with him at just about the time he hoped to pass the Moon.

But the outcome of the race was already being decided, ninety-two million miles away.

On Solar Observatory Three, far inside the orbit of Mercury, the automatic instruments recorded the whole history of the flare. A hundred million square miles of the Sun's surface suddenly exploded in such blue-white fury that, by comparison, the rest of the disk paled to a dull glow. Out of that seething inferno, twisting and turning like a living creature in the magnetic fields of its own creation, soared the electrified plasms of the great flare. Ahead of it, moving at the speed of light, went the warning flash of ultraviolet and X rays. That would reach Earth in eight minutes, and was relatively harmless. Not so the charged atoms that were following behind at their leisurely four million miles an hour—and which, in just over a day, would engulf *Diana*, *Lebedev*, and their accompanying little fleet in a cloud of lethal radiation.

The Commodore left his decision to the last possible minute. Even when the jet of plasma had been tracked past the orbit of Venus, there was a chance that it might miss the Earth. But when it was less than four hours away, and had already been picked up by the Moon-based radar network, he knew that there was no hope. All solar sailing was over for the next five or six years until the Sun was quiet again.

A great sigh of disappointment swept across the solar system. *Diana* and *Lebedev* were halfway between Earth and Moon,
running neck and neck—and now no one would ever know
which was the better boat. The enthusiasts would argue the
result for years; history would merely record: Race canceled
owing to solar storm.

When John Merton received the order, he felt a bitterness he
had not known since childhood. Across the years, sharp and
clear, came the memory of his tenth birthday. He had been
promised an exact scale model of the famous spaceship *Morning
Star*, and for weeks had been planning how he would assemble
it, where he would hang it up in his bedroom. And then, at the
last moment, his father had broken the news. "I'm sorry, John
—it costs too much money. Maybe next year . . ."

Half a century and a successful lifetime later, he was a
heartbroken boy again.

For a moment, he thought of disobeying the Commodore.
Suppose he sailed on, ignoring the warning? Even if the race
was abandoned, he could make a crossing to the Moon that
would stand in the record books for generations.

But that would be worse than stupidity. It would be
suicide—and a very unpleasant form of suicide. He had seen
men die of radiation poisoning, when the magnetic shielding of
their ships had failed in deep space. No—nothing was worth
that. . . .

He felt as sorry for Dimitri Markoff as for himself; they both
deserved to win, and now victory would go to neither. No man
could argue with the Sun in one of its rages, even though he
might ride upon its beams to the edge of space.

Only fifty miles astern now, the Commodore's launch was
drawing alongside *Lebedev*, preparing to take off her skipper.
There went the silver sail, as Dimitri—with feeling that he
would share—cut the rigging. The tiny capsule would be taken
back to Earth, perhaps to be used again—but a sail was spread for
one voyage only.

He could press the jettison button now, and save his res-
cuers a few minutes of time. But he could not do so. He wanted
to stay aboard to the very end, on the little boat that had been for

so long a part of his dreams and his life. The great sail was spread now at right angles to the Sun, exerting its utmost thrust. Long ago it had torn him clear of Earth—and *Diana* was still gaining speed.

Then, out of nowhere, beyond all doubt or hesitation, he knew what must be done. For the last time, he sat down before the computer that had navigated him halfway to the Moon.

When he had finished, he packed the log and his few personal belongings. Clumsily—for he was out of practice, and it was not an easy job to do by oneself—he climbed into the emergency survival suit.

He was just sealing the helmet when the Commodore's voice called over the radio. "We'll be alongside in five minutes, Captain. Please cut your sail so we won't foul it."

John Merton, first and last skipper of the sun-yacht *Diana*, hesitated for a moment. He looked for the last time around the tiny cabin, with its shining instruments and its neatly arranged controls, now all locked in their final positions. Then he said to the microphone: "I'm abandoning ship. Take your time to pick me up. *Diana* can look after herself."

There was no reply from the Commodore, and for that he was grateful. Professor van Stratten would have guessed what was happening—and would know that, in these final moments, he wished to be left alone.

He did not bother to exhaust the airlock, and the rush of escaping gas blew him gently out into space; the thrust he gave her then was his last gift to *Diana*. She dwindled away from him, sail glittering splendidly in the sunlight that would be hers for centuries to come. Two days from now she would flash past the Moon; but the Moon, like the Earth, could never catch her. Without his mass to slow her down, she would gain two thousand miles an hour in every day of sailing. In a month, she would be traveling faster than any ship that man had ever built.

As the Sun's rays weakened with distance, so her acceleration would fall. But even at the orbit of Mars, she would be gaining a thousand miles an hour in every day. Long before then, she would be moving too swiftly for the Sun itself to hold her.

Faster than any comet that had ever streaked in from the stars, she would be heading out into the abyss.

The glare of rockets, only a few miles away, caught Merton's eye. The launch was approaching to pick him up at thousands of times the acceleration that *Diana* could ever attain. But engines could burn for a few minutes only, before they exhausted their fuel—while *Diana* would still be gaining speed, driven outwards by the Sun's eternal fires, for ages yet to come.

"Good-bye, little ship," said John Merton. "I wonder what eyes will see you next, how many thousand years from now?"

At last he felt at peace, as the blunt torpedo of the launch nosed up beside him. He would never win the race to the Moon; but his would be the first of all man's ships to set sail on the long journey to the stars.

GEORGE R. R. MARTIN

The skill and strength displayed by today's
football players is often awesome to even the
most jaded spectator . . . but what might
happen if our football teams of the future
were to play against aliens from a far planet
where the gravity was so heavy that it produced beings who could simply run over
even the strongest human players? Would
teams from Earth stand any chance at all?

George R. R. Martin, a young man who has
become one of the top writers of science fiction in just a few years, tells of such a contest.
You can expect excitement—and surprises.

Run To
Starlight

Hill stared dourly at the latest free-fall football results from the Belt as they danced across the face of his desk console, but his mind was elsewhere. For the seventeenth time that week, he was silently cursing the stupidity and shortsightedness of the members of the Starport City Council.

The damn councilmen persisted in cutting the allocation for an artificial gravity grid out of the departmental budget every time Hill put it in. They had the nerve to tell him to stick to "traditional" sports in planning his recreational program for the year.

The old fools had no idea of the way free-fall football was catching on throughout the system, although he'd tried to explain it to them God knows how many times. The Belt sport should be an integral part of any self-respecting recreational program. And, on Earth, that meant you had to have a gravity grid. He'd planned on installing it beneath the stadium, but now—

The door to his office slid open with a soft hum. Hill looked up and frowned, snapping off the console. An agitated Jack De Angelis stepped through.

"What is it now?" Hill snapped.

"Uh, Rog, there's a guy here I think you better talk to," De Angelis replied. "He wants to enter a team in the City Football League."

"Registration closed on Tuesday," Hill said. "We've already got twelve teams. No room for any more. And why the hell

161

can't you handle this? You're in charge of the football program."

"This is a special case," De Angelis said.

"Then make an exception and let the team in if you want to," Hill interrupted. "Or don't let them in. It's your program. It's your decision. Must I be bothered with every bit of trivia in this whole damned department?"

"Hey, take it easy, Rog," De Angeles protested. "I don't know what you're so steamed up about. Look, I—hell, I'll show you the problem." He turned and went to the door. "Sir, would you step in here a minute," he said to someone outside.

Hill started to rise from his seat, but sank slowly back into the chair when the visitor appeared in the doorway.

De Angelis was smiling. "This is Roger Hill, the director of the Starport Department of Recreation," he said smoothly. "Rog, let me introduce Remjhard-nei, the head of the Brish'diri trade mission to Earth."

Hill rose again, and offered his hand numbly to the visitor. The Brish'dir was squat and grotesquely broad. He was a good foot shorter than Hill, who stood six four, but he still gave the impression of dwarfing the director somehow. A hairless, bullet-shaped head was set squarely atop the alien's massive shoulders. His eyes were glittering green marbles sunk in the slick, leathery gray skin. There were no external ears, only small holes on either side of the skull. The mouth was a lipless slash.

Diplomatically ignoring Hill's openmouthed stare, Remjhard bared his teeth in a quick smile and crushed the director's hand in his own. "I am most pleased to meet you, sir," he said in fluent English, his voice a deep bass growl. "I have come to enter a football team in the fine league your city so graciously runs."

Hill gestured for the alien to take a seat, and sat down himself. De Angelis, still smiling at his boss's stricken look, pulled another chair up to the desk for himself.

"Well, I—" Hill began, uncertainly. "This team, is it a—a Brish'diri team?"

Remjhard smiled again. "Yes," he answered. "Your football, it is a fine game. We of the mission have many times watched it being played on the 3-V wallscreens your people were so kind as to install. It has fascinated us. And now some of the half-men of our mission desire to try to play it." He reached slowly into the pocket of the black-and-silver uniform he wore, and pulled out a folded sheet of paper.

"This is a roster of our players," he said, handing it to Hill. "I believe the newsfax said such a list is required to enter your league."

Hill took the paper and glanced down at it uncertainly. It was a list of some fifteen Brish'diri names, neatly typed out. Everything seemed to be in order, but still—

"You'll forgive me, I hope," Hill said, "but I'm somewhat unfamiliar with the expressions of your people. You said —half-men? Do you mean children?"

Remjhard nodded, a quick inclination of his bulletlike head. "Yes. Male children, the sons of mission personnel. All are aged either eight or nine Earth seasons."

Hill silently sighed with relief. "I'm afraid it's out of the question, then," he said. "Mr. De Angelis said you were interested in the City League, but that league is for boys aged eighteen and up. Occasionally we'll admit a younger boy with exceptional talent and experience, but never anyone this young." He paused briefly. "We do have several leagues for younger boys, but they've already begun play. It's much too late to add another team at this point."

"Pardon, Director Hill, but I think you misunderstand," Remjhard said. "A Brish'diri male is fully mature at fourteen Earth years. In our culture, such a person is regarded as a full adult. A nine-year-old Brish'dir is roughly equivalent to an eighteen-year-old Terran male in terms of physical and intellectual development. That is why our half-men wish to register for this league and not one of the others, you see."

"He's correct, Rog," De Angelis said. "I've read a little about the Brish'diri, and I'm sure of it. In terms of maturity, these youngsters are eligible for the City League."

Hill threw De Angelis a withering glance. If there was one thing he didn't need at the moment, it was a Brish'diri football team in one of his leagues, and Remjhard was arguing convincingly enough without Jack's help.

"Well, all right," Hill said. "Your team may well be of age, but there are still problems. The Rec Department sports program is for local residents only. We simply don't have room to accommodate everyone who wants to participate. And your home planet is, as I understand, several hundred light-years beyond the Starport city limits." He smiled.

"True," Remjhard said. "But our trade mission has been in Starport for six years. An ideal location due to your city's proximity to Grissom Interstellar Spaceport, from which most of the Brish'diri traders operate while on Earth. All of the current members of the mission have been here for two Earth years, at least. We are Starport residents, Director Hill. I fail to understand how the location of Brishun enters into the matter at hand."

Hill squirmed uncomfortably in his seat, and glared at De Angelis, who was grinning. "Yes, you're probably right again," he said. "But I'm still afraid we won't be able to help you. Our junior leagues are touch football, but the City League, as you might know, is tackle. It can get quite rough at times. State safety regulations require the use of special equipment. To make sure no one is injured seriously. I'm sure you understand. And the Brish'diri . . ."

He groped for words, anxious not to offend. "The—uh —physical construction of the Brish'diri is so different from the Terran that our equipment couldn't possibly fit. Chances of injury would be too great, and the department would be liable. No. I'm sure it couldn't be allowed. Too much risk."

"We would provide special protective equipment," Remjhard said quietly. "We would never risk our own offspring if we did not feel it was safe."

Hill started to say something, stopped, and looked to De Angelis for help. He had run out of good reasons why the Brish'diri couldn't enter the league.

Jack smiled. "One problem remains, however," he said, coming to the director's rescue. "A bureaucratic snag, but a difficult one. Registration for the league closed on Tuesday. We've already had to turn away several teams, and if we make an exception in your case, well—" De Angelis shrugged. "Trouble. Complaints. I'm sorry, but we must apply the same rule to all."

Remjhard rose slowly from his seat, and picked up the roster from where it lay on the desk. "Of course," he said gravely. "All must follow the regulations. Perhaps next year we will be on time." He made a formal half-bow to Hill, turned, and walked from the office.

When he was sure the Brish'dir was out of earshot, Hill gave a heartfelt sigh and swiveled to face De Angelis. "That was close," he said. "Christ, a Baldy football team. Half the people in this town lost sons in the Brish'diri War, and they still hate them. I can imagine the complaints."

Hill frowned. "And you! Why couldn't you just get rid of him right away instead of putting me through that?"

De Angelis grinned. "Too much fun to pass up," he said. "I wondered if you'd figure out the right way to discourage him. The Brish'diri have an almost religious respect for laws, rules, and regulations. They wouldn't think of doing anything that would force someone to break a rule. In their culture, that's just as bad as breaking a rule yourself."

Hill nodded. "I would have remembered that myself if I hadn't been so paralyzed at the thought of a Brish'diri team in one of our leagues," he said limply. "And now that that's over with, I want to talk to you about that gravity grid. Do you think there's any way we could rent one instead of buying it outright? The Council might go for that. And I was thinking . . ."

A little over three hours later, Hill was signing some equipment requisitions when the office door slid open to admit a brawny, dark-haired man in a nondescript gray suit.

"Yes?" the director said, a trifle impatiently. "Can I help you?"

The dark-haired man flashed a government ID as he took a seat. "Maybe you can. But you certainly haven't so far, I'll tell you that much. My name's Tomkins. Mac Tomkins. I'm from the Federal E. T. Relations Board."

Hill groaned. "I suppose it's about that Brish'diri mess this morning," he said, shaking his head in resignation.

"Yes," Tomkins cut in at once. "We understand that the Brish'diri wanted to register some of their youngsters for a local football league. You forbade it on a technicality. We want to know why."

"Why?" said Hill incredulously, staring at the government man. "Why? For God's sakes, the Brish'diri War was only over seven years ago. Half of those boys on our football teams had brothers killed by the Bulletbrains. Now you want me to tell them to play football with the subhuman monsters of seven years back? They'd run me out of town."

Tomkins grimaced, and looked around the room. "Can that door be locked?" he asked, pointing to the door he had come in by.

"Of course," Hill replied, puzzled.

"Lock it then," Tomkins said. Hill adjusted the appropriate control on his desk.

"What I'm going to tell you should not go beyond this room," Tomkins began.

Hill cut him off with a snort. "Oh, come now, Mr. Tomkins. I may be only a small-time sports official, but I'm not stupid. You're hardly about to impart some galaxy-shattering top secret to a man you met a few seconds ago."

Tomkins smiled. "True. The information's not secret, but it is a little ticklish. We would prefer that every Joe in the street doesn't know about it."

"All right, I'll buy that for now. Now what's this all about? I'm sorry if I've got no patience with subtlety, but the most difficult problem I've handled in the last year was the protest in the championship game in the Class B Soccer League. Diplomacy just isn't my forte."

"I'll be brief," Tomkins said. "We—E. T. Relations, that is—we want you to admit the Brish'diri team into your football league."

"You realize the furor it would cause?" Hill asked.

"We have some idea. In spite of that, we want them admitted."

"Why, may I ask?"

"Because of the furor if they aren't admitted." Tomkins paused to stare at Hill for a second, then apparently reached a decision of some sort and continued. "The Earth-Brishun War was a ghastly, bloody deadlock, although our propaganda men insist on pretending it was a great victory. No sane man on either side wants it resumed. But not everyone is sane."

The agent frowned in distaste. "There are elements among us who regard the Brish'diri—or the Bulletbrains, or Baldies, or whatever you want to call them—as monsters, even now, seven years after the killing has ended."

"And you think a Brish'diri football team would help to overcome the leftover hates?" Hill interrupted.

"Partially. But that's not the important part. You see, there is also an element among the Brish'diri that regards humans as subhuman—vermin to be wiped from the galaxy. They are a very virile, competitive race. Their whole culture stresses combat. The dissident element I mentioned will seize on your refusal to admit a Brish'diri team as a sign of fear, an admission of human inferiority. They'll use it to agitate for a resumption of the war. We don't want to risk giving them a propaganda victory like that. Relations are too strained as it is."

"But the Brish'dir I spoke to—" Hill objected. "I explained it all to him. A rule. Surely their respect for law—"

"Remjhard-nei is a leader of the Brish'diri peace faction. He personally will defend your position. But he and his son were disappointed by the refusal. They will talk. They already have been talking. And that means that eventually the war faction will get hold of the story and turn it against us."

"I see. But what can I do at this point? I've already told Remjhard that registration closed Tuesday. If I understand correctly, his own morality would never permit him to take advantage of an exception now."

Tomkins nodded. "True. You can't make an exception. Just change the rule. Let in all the teams you refused. Expand the league."

Hill shook his head, wincing. "But our budget—it couldn't take it. We'd have more games. We'd need more time, more referees, more equipment."

Tomkins dismissed the problem with a wave of his hand.

"The government is already buying the Brish'diri special football uniforms. We'd be happy to cover all your extra costs. You'd get a better recreational program for all concerned."

Hill still looked doubtful. "Well . . ."

"Moreover," Tomkins said, "we might be able to arrange a government grant or two to bolster other improvements in your program. Now how about it?"

Hill's eyes sparkled with sudden interest. "A grant? How big a grant? Could you swing a gravity grid?"

"No problem," said Tomkins. A slow grin spread across his face.

Hill returned the grin. "Then, mister, Starport's got itself a Brish'diri football team. But, oh, are they going to scream!" He flicked on the desk intercom. "Get Jack De Angelis in here," he ordered. "I've got a little surprise for him."

The sky above Starport Municipal Stadium was bleak and dreary on a windy Saturday morning a week later, but Hill didn't mind it at all. The stadium force bubble kept out the thin, wet drizzle that had soaked him to the bones on the way to the game, and the weather fitted his mood beautifully.

Normally, Hill was far too busy to attend any of his department's sporting events. Normally *everyone* was too busy to attend the department's sporting events. The Rec Department leagues got fairly good coverage in the local newspaper, but they seldom drew many spectators. The record was something like four hundred people for a championship game a few years ago.

Or rather, that *was* the record, Hill reminded himself. No more. The stadium was packed today, in spite of the hour, the rain, and everything else. Municipal Stadium was never packed except for the traditional Thanksgiving Day football game between Starport High and its archrival, Grissom City Prep. But today it was packed.

Hill knew why. It had been drilled into him the hard way after he had made the damn-fool decision to let the Brish-diri into the league. The whole city was up in arms. Six local teams had withdrawn from the City League rather than play with the "inhuman monsters." The office switchboard had been flooded with calls daily, the vast majority of them angry denunciations of Hill. A city council member had called for his resignation.

And that, Hill reflected glumly, was probably what it would come to in the end. The local newspaper, which had always been hard-line conservative on foreign affairs, was backing the drive to force Hill out of office. One of its editorials had reminded him gleefully that Starport Municipal Stadium was dedicated to those who had given their lives in the Brish'diri War, and had screamed about "desecration." Meanwhile, on its sports pages, the paper had taken to calling the Brish-diri team "the Baldy Eagles."

Hill squirmed uncomfortably in his seat on the fifty-yard line, and prayed silently that the game would begin. He could feel the angry stares on the back of his neck, and he had the uneasy impression that he was going to be hit with a rock any second now.

Across the field, he could see the camera installation of one of the big 3-V networks. All five of them were here, of course; the game had gotten planetwide publicity. The newsfax wires had also sent reporters, although they had seemed a little confused about what kind of a story this was. One had sent a political reporter, the other a sportswriter.

Out on the stadium's artificial grass, the human team was running through a few plays and warming up. Their bright-red uniforms were emblazoned with KEN'S COMPUTER REPAIR in white lettering, and they wore matching white helmets. They looked pretty good, Hill decided from watching them practice, although they were far from championship caliber. Still, against a team that had never played football before, they should mop up.

De Angelis, wearing a pained expression and a ref's striped shirt, was out on the field talking to his officials. Hill was taking no chances with bad calls in this game. He'd made sure the department's best men were on hand to officiate.

Tomkins was also there, sitting in the stands a few sections away from Hill. But the Brish'diri were not. Remjhard wanted to attend, but E. T. Relations, on Hill's advice, had told him to stay at the mission. Instead, the game was being piped to him over closed-circuit 3-V.

Hill suddenly straightened in his seat. The Brish'diri team, which called itself the Kosg-Anjehn after a flying carnivore native to Brishun, had arrived, and the players were walking slowly out onto the field.

There was a brief instant of silence, and then someone in the crowd started booing. Others picked it up. Then others. The stadium was filled with the boos. Although, Hill noted with relief, not everyone was joining in. Maybe there were some people who saw things his way.

The Brish'diri ignored the catcalls. Or seemed to, at any rate. Hill had never seen an angry Brish'dir, and was unsure how one would go about showing his anger.

The Kosg-Anjehn wore tight-fitting black uniforms, with odd-looking elongated silver helmets to cover their bullet-shaped heads. They looked like no football team Hill had ever seen. Only a handful of them stood over five feet, but they were all as squat and broad as a tackle for the Packers. Their arms and legs were thick and stumpy, but rippled with muscles that bulged in the wrong places. The helmeted heads, however, gave an impression of frailty, like eggshells ready to shatter at the slightest impact.

Two of the Brish-diri detached themselves from the group and walked over to De Angelis. Evidently they felt they didn't need a warm-up, and wanted to start immediately. De Angelis talked to them for an instant, then turned and beckoned to the captain of the human team.

"How do you think it'll go?"

Hill turned. It was Tomkins. The E. T. agent had struggled through the crowd to his side.

"Hard to say," the director replied. "The Brish'diri have never really played football before, so the odds are they'll lose. Being from a heavy-gravity planet, they'll be stronger than the humans, so that might give them an edge. But they're also a lot slower, from what I hear."

"I'll have to root them home," Tomkins said with a smile.

"Bolster the cause of interstellar relations and all that."

Hill scowled. "You root them home if you like. I'm pulling for the humans. Thanks to you, I'm in enough trouble already. If they catch me rooting for the Brish'diri they'll tear me to shreds."

He turned his attention back to the field. The Computermen had won the toss, and elected to receive. One of the taller Brish'diri was going back to kick off.

"Tuhgayh-dei," Tomkins provided helpfully. "The son of the mission's chief linguist." Hill nodded.

Tuhgayh-dei ran forward with a ponderous, lumbering gallop, nearly stopped when he finally reached the football, and slammed his foot into it awkwardly but hard. The ball landed in the upper tier of the stands, and a murmur went through the crowd.

"Pretty good," Tomkins said. "Don't you think?"

"Too good," replied Hill. He did not elaborate.

The humans took the ball on their twenty. The Computermen went into a huddle, broke it with a loud clap, and ran to their positions. A ragged cheer went up from the stands.

The humans went down into the three-point stance. Their Brish'diri opponents did not. The alien linemen just stood there, hands dangling at their sides, crouching a little.

"They don't know much about football," Hill said. "But after that kickoff, I wonder if they have to."

The ball was snapped, and the quarterback for Ken's Computer Repair, a rangy ex-high-school star named Sullivan, faded back to pass. The Brish'diri rushed forward in a crude blitz, and crashed into the human linemen.

An instant later, Sullivan was lying face down in the grass, buried under three Brish'diri. The aliens had blown through the offensive line as if it didn't exist.

That made it second-and-fifteen. The humans huddled again, came out to another cheer, not quite so loud as the first one. The ball was snapped. Sullivan handed off to a beefy fullback, who crashed straight ahead.

One of the Brish-diri brought him down before he went half

a yard. It was a clumsy tackle, around the shoulders. But the force of the contact knocked the fullback several yards in the wrong direction.

When the humans broke from their huddle for the third time the cheer could scarcely be heard. Again Sullivan tried to pass. Again the Brish'diri blasted through the line en masse. Again Sullivan went down for a loss.

Hill groaned. "This looks worse every minute," he said.

Tomkins didn't agree. "I don't think so. They're doing fine. What difference does it make who wins?"

Hill didn't bother to answer that.

There was no cheering when the humans came out in punt formation. Once more the Brish'diri put on a strong rush, but the punter got the ball away before they reached him.

It was a good, deep kick. The Kosg-Anjehn took over on their own twenty-five yard line. Marhdain-nei, Remjhard's son, was the Brish'diri quarterback. On the first play from scrimmage, he handed off to a halfback, a runt built like a tank.

The Brish'diri blockers flattened their human opponents almost effortlessly, and the runt plowed through the gaping hole, ran over two would-be tacklers, and burst into the clear. He was horribly slow, however, and the defenders finally brought him down from behind after a modest thirty-yard gain. But it took three people to stop him.

On the next play, Marhdain tried to pass. He got excellent protection, but his receivers, trudging along at top speed, had defensemen all over them. And the ball, when thrown, went sizzling over the heads of Brish'diri and humans alike.

Marhdain returned to the ground again after that, and handed off to a runt halfback once more. This time he tried to sweep around end, but was hauled to the ground after a gain of only five yards by a quartet of human tacklers.

That made it third-and-five. Marhdain kept to the ground. He gave the ball to his other halfback, and the brawny Brish'dir smashed up the middle. He was a little bit faster than the runt. When he got in the clear, only one man managed to catch him from behind. And one wasn't enough. The alien shrugged off the tackle and lumbered on across the goal line.

The extra point try went under the crossbar instead of over it. But it still nearly killed the poor guy in the stands who tried to catch the ball.

Tomkins was grinning. Hill shook his head in disgust. "This isn't the way it's supposed to go," he said. "They'll kill us if the Brish'diri win."

The kickoff went out of the stadium entirely this time. On the first play from the twenty, a Brish'diri lineman roared through the line and hit Sullivan just as he was handing off. Sullivan fumbled.

Another Brish'dir picked up the loose ball and carried it into the end zone while most of the humans were still lying on the ground.

"My god," said Hill, feeling a bit numb. "They're too strong. They're too damn strong. The humans can't cope with their strength. Can't stop them."

"Cheer up," said Tomkins. "It can't get much worse for your side."

But it did. It got a lot worse.

On offense, the Brish'diri were well-nigh unstoppable. Their runners were all short on speed, but made up for it with muscle. On play after play, they smashed straight up the middle behind a wall of blockers, flicking tacklers aside like bothersome insects.

And then Marhdain began to hit on his passes. Short passes, of course. The Brish'diri lacked the speed to cover much ground. But they could outjump any human, and they snared pass after pass in the air. There was no need to worry about interceptions. The humans simply couldn't hang on to Marhdain's smoking pitches.

On defense, things were every bit as bad. The Computermen couldn't run against the Brish'diri line. And Sullivan seldom had time to complete a pass, for the alien rushers were unstoppable. The few passes he did hit on went for touchdowns; no Brish'diri could catch a human from behind. But those were few and far between.

When Hill fled the stadium in despair at the half, the score was Kosg-Anjehn 37, Ken's Computer Repair 7.

The final score was 57 to 14. The Brish'diri had emptied their bench in the second half.

Hill didn't have the courage to attend the next Brish'diri game later in the week. But nearly everyone else in the city showed up to see if the Kosg-Anjehn could do it again.

They did. In fact, they did even better. They beat Anderson's Drugs by a lopsided 61 to 9 score.

After the Brish'diri won their third contest, 43 to 17, the huge crowds began tapering off. The Starport Municipal Stadium was only three quarters full when the Kosg-Anjehn rolled over the Stardusters, 38 to 0, and a mere handful showed up on a rainy Thursday afternoon to see the aliens punish the United Veterans Association, 51 to 6. And no one came after that.

For Hill, the Brish'diri win over the UVA-sponsored team was the final straw. The local paper made a heyday out of that, going on and on about the "ironic injustice" of having the UVA slaughtered by the Brish'diri in a stadium dedicated to the dead veterans of the Brish'diri War. And Hill, of course, was the main villain in the piece.

The phone calls had finally let up by that point. But the mail had been flowing into his office steadily, and most of it was not very comforting. The harassed Rec director got a few letters of commendation and support, but the bulk of the flood speculated crudely about his ancestry or threatened his life and property.

Two more city councilmen had come out publicly in favor of Hill's dismissal after the Brish'diri defeated UVA. Several others on the council were wavering, while Hill's supporters, who backed him strongly in private, were afraid to say anything for the record. The municipal elections were simply too close, and none were willing to risk their political skins.

And of course the assistant director of recreation, next in line for Hill's job, had wasted no time in saying *he* would certainly never have done such an unpatriotic thing.

With disaster piling upon disaster, it was only natural that Hill reacted with something less than enthusiasm when he walked into his office a few days after the fifth Kosg-Anjehn victory and found Tomkins sitting at his desk waiting for him.

"And what in the hell do you want now?" Hill roared at the E. T. Relations man.

Tomkins looked slightly abashed, and got up from the director's chair. He had been watching the latest free-fall football results on the desk console while waiting for Hill to arrive.

"I've got to talk to you," Tomkins said. "We've got a problem."

"We've got lots of problems," Hill replied. He strode angrily to his desk, sat down, flicked off the console, and pulled a sheaf of papers from a drawer.

"This is the latest of them," he continued, waving the papers at Tompkins. "One of the kids broke his leg in the Starduster game. It happens all the time. Football's a rough game. You can't do anything to prevent it. On a normal case, the department would send a letter of apology to the parents, our insurance would pay for it, and everything would be forgotten.

"But not in this case. Oh, no. This injury was inflicted while the kid was playing against the Brish'diri. So his parents are charging negligence on our part and suing the city. So our insurance company refuses to pay up. It claims the policy doesn't cover damage by inhuman, superstrong, alien monsters. Bah! How's that for a problem, Mr. Tomkins? Plenty more where that came from."

Tomkins frowned. "Very unfortunate. But my problem is a lot more serious than that." Hill started to interrupt, but the E. T. Relations man waved him down. "No, please, hear me out. This is very important."

He looked around for a seat, grabbed the nearest chair, and pulled it up to the desk. "Our plans have backfired badly," he began. "There has been a serious miscalculation—our fault entirely, I'm afraid. E. T. Relations failed to consider *all* the ramifications of this Brish'diri football team."

Hill fixed him with an iron stare. "What's wrong now?"

"Well, Tompkins said awkwardly, "we knew that refusal to admit the Kosg-Anjehn into your league would be a sign of human weakness and fear to the Brish'diri war faction. But once you admitted them, we thought the problem was solved.

"It wasn't. We went wrong when we assumed that winning or losing would make no difference to the Brish'diri. To us, it was just a game. Didn't matter who won. After all, Brish'diri and Terrans would be getting to know each other, competing harmlessly on even terms. Nothing but good could come from it, we felt."

"So?" Hill interrupted. "Get to the point."

Tomkins shook his head sadly. "The point is, we didn't know the Brish'diri would win so *big*. And so *regularly*." He paused. "We—uh—we got a transmission late last night from one of our men on Brishun. It seems the Brish'diri war faction is using the one-sided football scores as propaganda to prove the racial inferiority of humans. They seem to be getting a lot of mileage out of it."

Hill winced. "So it was all for nothing. So I've subjected myself to all this abuse and endangered my career for absolutely nothing. Great! That was all I needed, I tell you."

"We still might be able to salvage something," Tomkins said. "That's why I came to see you. If you can arrange it for the Brish'diri to *lose*, it would knock holes in that superiority yarn and make the war faction look like fools. It would discredit them for quite a while."

"And just how am I supposed to *arrange* for them to lose, as you so nicely put it? What do you think I'm running here anyway, professional wrestling?"

Tomkins just shrugged lamely. "I was hoping you'd have some ideas," he said.

Hill leaned forward, and flicked on his intercom. "Is Jack out there?" he asked. "Good. Send him in."

The lanky sports official appeared less than a minute later. "You're on top of this City football mess," Hill said. "What's the chances the Kosg-Anjehn will lose?"

De Angelis looked puzzled. "Not all that good, offhand," he replied. "They've got a damn fine team."

He reached into his back pocket and pulled out a notebook. "Let me check their schedule," he continued, thumbing through the pages. He stopped when he found the place.

"Well, the league's got a round-robin schedule, as you

know. Every team plays every other team once, best record is champion. Now the Brish'diri are currently five to zero, and they've beaten a few of the better teams. We've got ten teams left in the league, so they've got four games left to play. Only, two of those are with the weakest teams in the league, and the third opponent is only mediocre."

"And the fourth?" Hill said hopefully.

"That's your only chance. An outfit sponsored by a local tavern, the Blastoff Inn. Good team. Fast, strong. Plenty of talent. They're also five to zero, and should give the Brish'diri some trouble." De Angelis frowned. "But, to be frank, I've seen both teams, and I'd still pick the Brish'diri. That ground game of theirs is just too much." He snapped the notebook shut and pocketed it again.

"Would a close game be good enough?" Hill said, turning to Tomkins again.

The E. T. Relations man shook his head. "No. They have to be beaten. If they lose, the whole season's meaningless. Proves nothing but that the two races can compete on roughly equal terms. But if they win, it looks like they're invincible, and our stature in Brish'diri eyes takes a nose dive."

"Then they'll have to lose, I guess," Hill said. His gaze shifted back to De Angelis. "Jack, you and me are going to have to do some hard thinking about how the Kosg-Anjehn can be beaten. And then we're going to call up the manager of the Blastoff Inn team and give him a few tips. You have any ideas?"

De Angelis scratched his head thoughtfully. "Well—" he began. "Maybe we—"

During the weeks that followed, De Angelis met with the Blastoff Inn coach regularly to discuss plans and strategy, and supervised a few practice sessions. Hill, meanwhile, was fighting desperately to keep his job, and jotting down ideas on how to beat the Brish'diri during every spare moment.

Untouched by the furor, The Kosg-Anjehn won its sixth game handily, 40 to 7, and then rolled to devastating victories over the circuit's two cellar-dwellers. The margins were 73 to 0 and 62 to 7. That gave them an unblemished 8 to 0 ledger, with one game left to play.

But the Blastoff Inn team was also winning regularly, although never as decisively. It too would enter the last game of the season undefeated.

The local paper heralded the showdown with a sports-page streamer on the day before the game. The lead opened, "The stakes will be high for the entire human race tomorrow at Municipal Stadium, when Blastoff Inn meets the Brish'diri Baldy Eagles for the championship of the Department of Recreation City Football League."

The reporter who wrote the story never dreamed how close to the truth he actually was.

The crowds returned to the stadium for the championship game, although they fell far short of a packed house. The local paper was there too. But the 3-V networks and the newsfax wires were long gone. The novelty of the story had worn off quickly.

Hill arrived late, just before game time, and joined Tomkins on the fifty-yard line. The E. T. agent seemed to have cheered up somewhat. "Our guys looked pretty good during the warm-up," he told the director. "I think we've got a chance."

His enthusiasm was not catching, however. "Blastoff Inn might have a chance, but I sure don't," Hill said glumly. "The city council is meeting tonight to consider a motion for calling for my dismissal. I have a strong suspicion that it's going to pass, no matter who wins this afternoon."

"Hmmmm," said Tomkins, for want of anything better to say. "Just ignore the old fools. Look, the game's starting."

Hill muttered something under his breath and turned his attention back to the field. The Brish'diri had lost the toss once more, and the kickoff had once again soared out of the stadium. It was first-and-ten for Blastoff Inn on its own twenty.

And at that point the script suddenly changed.

The humans lined up for their first play of the game but with a difference. Instead of playing immediately in back of the center, the Blastoff quarterback was several yards deep, in a shotgun formation.

The idea, Hill recalled, was to take maximum advantage of human speed, and mount a strong passing offense. Running against the Brish'diri was all but impossible, he and De Angelis had concluded after careful consideration. That meant an aerial attack, and the only way to provide that was to give the Blastoff quarterback time to pass. Ergo, the shotgun formation.

The hike from center was dead on target and the Blastoff receivers shot off downfield, easily outpacing the ponderous Brish'diri defensemen. As usual, the Kosg-Anjehn crashed through the line en masse, but they had covered only half the distance to the quarterback before he got off the pass.

It was a long bomb, a psychological gambit to shake up the Brish'diri by scoring on the first play of the game. Unfortunately, the pass was slightly overthrown.

Hill swore.

It was now second-and-ten. Again the humans lined up in a shotgun offense, and again the Blastoff quarterback got off the pass in time. It was a short, quick pitch to the sideline, complete for a nine-yard gain. The crowd cheered lustily.

Hill wasn't sure what the Brish'diri would expect on third-and-one. But whatever it was, they didn't get it. With the aliens still slightly off balance, Blastoff went for the bomb again.

This time it was complete. All alone in the open, the fleet human receiver snagged the pass neatly and went all the way in for the score. The Brish'diri never laid a hand on him.

The crowd sat in stunned silence for a moment when the pass was caught. Then, when it became clear that there was no way to prevent the score, the cheering began, and peaked slowly to an ear-splitting roar. The stadium rose to its feet as one, screaming wildly.

For the first time all season, the Kosg-Anjehn trailed. A picture-perfect place kick made the score 7 to 0 in favor of Blastoff Inn.

Tomkins was on his feet, cheering loudly. Hill, who had remained seated, regarded him dourly. "Sit down," he said. "The game's not over yet."

The Brish'diri soon underlined that point. No sooner did they take over the ball than they came pounding back upfield, smashing into the line again and again. The humans alternated between a dozen different defensive formations. None of them seemed to do any good. The Brish'diri steamroller ground ahead inexorably.

The touchdown was an anticlimax. Luckily, however, the extra point try failed. Tuhgayh-dei lost a lot of footballs, but he had still not developed a knack for putting his kicks between the crossbars.

The Blastoff offense took the field again. They looked determined. The first play from scrimmage was a short pass over the middle, complete for fifteen yards. Next came a tricky double pass. Complete for twelve yards.

On the following play, the Blastoff fullback tried to go up the middle. He got creamed for a five-yard loss.

"If they stop our passing, we're dead," Hill said to Tomkins, without taking his eyes off the field.

Luckily, the Blastoff quarterback quickly gave up on the idea of establishing a running game. A prompt return to the air gave the humans another first down. Three plays later, they scored. Again the crowd roared.

Trailing now 14 to 6, the Brish'diri once more began to pound their way upfield. But the humans, elated by their lead, were a little tougher now. Reading the Brish'diri offense with confident precision, the defensemen began gang-tackling the alien runners.

The Kosg-Anjehn drive slowed down, then stalled. They were forced to surrender the ball near the fifty-yard line.

Tomkins started pounding Hill on the back. "You did it," he said. "We stopped them on offense too. We're going to win."

"Take it easy," Hill replied. "That was a fluke. Several of our men just happened to be in the right place at the right time. It's happened before. No one ever said the Brish'diri scored every time they got the ball. Only most of the time."

Back on the field, the Blastoff passing attack was still humming smoothly. A few accurate throws put the humans on the Kosg-Anjehn's thirty.

And then the aliens changed formations. They took several men off the rush, and put them on pass defense. They started double-teaming the Blastoff receivers. Except it wasn't normal double-teaming. The second defender was playing far back of the line of scrimmage. By the time the human had outrun the first Brish'dir, the second would be right on top of him.

"I was afraid of something like this," Hill said. "We're not the only ones who can react to circumstances."

The Blastoff quarterback ignored the shift in the alien defense, and stuck to his aerial game plan. But his first pass from the thirty, dead on target, was batted away by a Brish'dir defender who happened to be right on top of the play.

The same thing happened on second down. That made it third-and-ten. The humans called time out. There was a hurried conference on the sidelines.

When action resumed, the Blastoff offense abandoned the shotgun formation. Without the awesome Brish'diri blitz to worry about, the quarterback was relatively safe in his usual position.

There was a quick snap, and the quarterback got rid of the ball equally quickly, an instant before a charging Brish'dir bore him to the ground. The halfback who got the handoff streaked to the left in an end run.

The other Brish'diri defenders lumbered towards him en masse to seal shut the sideline. But just as he reached the sideline, still behind the line of scrimmage, the Blastoff halfback handed off to a teammate streaking right.

A wide grin spread across Hill's face. A reverse!

The Brish'diri were painfully slow to change directions. The human swept around right end with ridiculous ease and shot upfield, surrounded by blockers. The remaining Brish'diri closed in. One or two were taken out by team blocks. The rest found it impossible to lay their hands on the swift, darting runner. Dodging this way and that, he wove a path neatly between them and loped into the end zone.

Once more the stadium rose to its feet. This time Hill stood up too.

Tomkins was beaming again. "Ha!" he said. "I thought you were the one who said we couldn't run against them."

"Normally we can't," the director replied. "There's no way to run over or through them, so runs up the middle are out. End runs are better, but if they're in their formal formation, that too is a dreary prospect. There is no way a human runner can get past a wall of charging Brish'diri.

"However, when they spread out like they just did, they give us an open field to work with. We can't go over or through them, no, but we sure as hell can go *between* them when they're scattered all over the field. And Blastoff Inn has several excellent open-field runners."

The crowd interrupted him with another roar to herald a successful extra-point conversion. It was now 21 to 6.

The game was far from over, however. The human defense was not nearly as successful on the next series of downs. Instead of relying exclusively on the running game, Marhdain-nei kept his opponents guessing with some of his patented short, hard pop passes.

To put on a more effective rush, the Blastoff defense spread out at wide intervals. The offensive line thus opened up, and several humans managed to fake out slower Brish'diri blockers and get past them to the quarterback. Marhdain was even thrown for a loss once.

But the Blastoff success was short-lived. Marhdain adjusted quickly. The widely spread human defense, highly effective against the pass, was a total failure against the run. The humans were too far apart to gang-tackle. And there was no way short of mass assault to stop a Brish'dir in full stride.

After that there was no stopping the Kosg-Anjehn, as Marhdain alternated between the pass and the run according to the human defensive formation. The aliens marched upfield quickly for their second touchdown.

This time, even the extra point was on target.

The Brish'diri score had taken some of the steam out of the crowd, but the Blastoff Inn offense showed no signs of being disheartened when they took the field again. With the aliens back in their original blitz defense, the human quarterback fell back on the shotgun once more.

His first pass was overthrown, but the next three in a row were dead on target and moved Blastoff to the Kosg-Anjehn forty. A running play, inserted to break the monotony, ended in a six-yard loss. Then came another incomplete pass. The toss was perfect, but the receiver dropped the ball.

That made it third-and-ten, and a tremor of apprehension went through the crowd. Nearly everyone in the stadium realized that the humans had to keep scoring to stay in the game.

The snap from center was quick and clean. The Blastoff quarterback snagged the ball, took a few unhurried steps backward to keep at a safe distance from the oncoming Brish'diri rushers, and tried to pick out a receiver. He scanned the field carefully. Then he reared back and unleashed a bomb.

It looked like another touchdown. The human had his alien defender beaten by a good five yards and was still gaining ground. The pass was a beauty.

But then, as the ball began to spiral downward, the Brish'diri defender stopped suddenly in midstride. Giving up his hopeless chase, he craned his head around to look for the ball, spotted it, braced himself—and jumped.

Brish'diri leg muscles, evolved for the heavy gravity of Brishun, were far more powerful than their human counterparts. Despite their heavier bodies, the Brish'diri could easily outjump any human. But so far they had only taken advantage of that fact to snare Marhdain's pop passes.

But now, as Hill blinked in disbelief, the Kosg-Anjehn defenseman leaped at least five feet into the air to meet the descending ball in midair and knock it aside with a vicious backhand slap.

The stadium moaned.

Forced into a punting situation, Blastoff Inn suddenly seemed to go limp. The punter fumbled the snap from center, and kicked the ball away when he tried to pick it up. The Brish'dir who picked it up got twenty yards before he was brought down.

The human defense this time put up only token resistance as Marhdain led his team downfield on a series of short passes and devastating runs.

It took the Brish'diri exactly six plays to narrow the gap to 21 to 19. Luckily, Tuhgayh missed another extra point.

There was a loud cheer when the Blastoff offense took the field again. But right from the first play after the kickoff, it was obvious that something had gone out of them.

The human quarterback, who had been giving a brilliant performance, suddenly became erratic. To add to his problems, the Brish'diri were suddenly jumping all over the field.

The alien kangeroo-pass defense had several severe limitations. It demanded precise timing and excellent reflexes on the part of the jumpers, neither of which was a Brish'diri forte. But it was a disconcerting tactic that the Blastoff quarterback had never come up against before. He didn't know quite how to cope with it.

The humans drove to their own forty, bogged down, and were forced to punt. The Kosg-Anjehn promptly marched the ball back the other way and scored. For the first time in the game, they led.

The next Blastoff drive was a bit more successful, and reached the Brish'diri twenty before it ground to a halt. The humans salvaged the situation with a field goal.

The Kosg-Anjehn rolled up another score, driving over the goal line just seconds before the half ended.

The score stood at 31 to 24 in favor of the Brish'diri.

And there was no secret about the way the tide was running.

It had grown very quiet in the stands.

Tomkins, wearing a worried expression, turned to Hill with a sigh. "Well, maybe we'll make a comeback in the second half. We're only down seven. That's not so bad."

"Maybe," Hill said doubtfully. "But I don't think so. They've got all the momentum. I hate to say so, but I think we're going to get run out of the stadium in the second half."

Tomkins frowned. "I certainly hope not. I'd hate to see what the Brish'diri war faction would do with a really lopsided score. Why, they'd—" He stopped, suddenly aware that Hill wasn't paying the slightest bit of attention. The director's eyes had wandered back to the field.

"Look," Hill said, pointing. "By the gate. Do you see what I see?"

"It looks like a car from the trade mission," the E. T. agent said, squinting to make it out.

"And who's that getting out?"

Tomkins hesitated. "Remjhard-nei," he said at last.

The Brish'dir climbed smoothly from the low-slung black vehicle, walked a short distance across the stadium grass, and vanished through the door leading to one of the dressing rooms.

"What's he doing here?" Hill asked. "Wasn't he supposed to stay away from the games?"

Tomkins scratched his head uneasily. "Well, that's what we advised. Especially at first, when hostility was at its highest. But he's not a *prisoner*, you know. There's no way we could force him to stay away from the games if he wants to attend."

Hill was frowning. "Why should he take your advice all season and suddenly disregard it now?"

Tomkins shrugged. "Maybe he wanted to see his son win a championship."

"Maybe. But I don't think so. There's something funny going on here."

By the time the second half was ready to begin, Hill was feeling even more apprehensive. The Kosg-Anjehn had taken the field a few minutes earlier, but Remjhard had not reappeared. He was still down in the alien locker room.

Moreover, there was something subtly different about the Brish'diri as they lined up to receive the kickoff. Nothing drastic. Nothing obvious. But somehow the atmosphere was changed. The aliens appeared more carefree, more relaxed. Almost as if they had stopped taking their opponents seriously.

Hill could sense the difference. He'd seen other teams with the same sort of attitude before, in dozens of other contests. It was the attitude of a team that already knows how the game is going to come out. The attitude of a team that knows it is sure to win—or doomed to lose.

The kickoff was poor and wobbly. A squat Brish'dir took it near the thirty and headed upfield. Two Blastoff tacklers met him at the thirty-five.

He fumbled.

The crowd roared. For a second the ball rolled loose on the stadium grass. A dozen hands reached for it, knocking it this way and that. Finally, a brawny Blastoff lineman landed squarely on top of it and trapped it beneath him.

And suddenly the game turned around again.

"I don't believe it," Hill said. "That was it. The break we needed. After that touchdown pass was knocked aside, our team just lost heart. But now, after this, look at them. We're back in this game."

The Blastoff offense raced onto the field, broke the huddle with an enthusiastic shout, and lined up. It was first-and-ten from the Brish'diri twenty-eight.

The first pass was deflected off a bounding Brish'dir. The second, however, went for a touchdown.

The score was tied.

The Kosg-Anjehn held on to the kickoff this time. They put the ball in play near the twenty-five.

Marhdain opened the series of downs with a pass. No one, human or Brish'dir, was within ten yards of where it came down. The next play was a run. But the Kosg-Anjehn halfback hesitated oddly after he took the handoff. Given time to react, four humans smashed into him at the line of scrimmage. Marhdain went back to the air. The pass was incomplete again.

The Brish'diri were forced to punt.

Up in the stands, Tomkins was laughing wildly. He began slapping Hill on the back again. "Look at that! Not even a first down. We held them. And you said they were going to run us out of the stadium."

A strange half-smile danced across the director's face. "Ummm," he said. "So I did." The smile faded.

It was a good, solid punt, but Blastoff's deep man fielded it superbly and ran it back to the fifty. From there, it took only seven plays for the human quarterback, suddenly looking cool and confident again, to put the ball in the end zone.

Bouncing Brish'diri had evidently ceased to disturb him. He simply threw the ball through spots where they did not happen to be bouncing.

This time the humans missed the extra point. But no one

cared. The score was 37 to 31. Blastoff Inn was ahead again.

And they were ahead to stay. No sooner had the Kosg-Anjehn taken over again than Marhdain threw an interception. It was the first interception he had thrown all season.

Naturally, it was run back for a touchdown.

After that, the Brish'diri seemed to revive a little. They drove three quarters of the way down the field, but then they bogged down as soon as they got within the shadow of the goal posts. On fourth-and-one from the twelve-yard line, the top Brish'diri runner slipped and fell behind the line of scrimmage.

Blastoff took over. And scored.

From then on, it was more of the same.

The final score was 56 to 31. The wrong team had been run out of the stadium.

Tomkins, of course, was in ecstasy. "We did it. I knew we could do it. This is perfect, just perfect. We humiliated them. The war faction will be totally discredited now. They'll never be able to stand up under the ridicule." He grinned and slapped Hill soundly on the back once again.

Hill winced under the blow, and eyed the E. T. man dourly. "There's something funny going on here. If the Brish'diri had played all season the way they played in the second half, they never would have gotten this far. Something happened in that locker room during half-time."

Nothing could dent Tomkins' grin, however. "No, no," he said. "It was the fumble. That was what did it. It demoralized them, and they fell apart. They just clutched, that's all. It happens all the time."

"Not to teams this good it doesn't," Hill replied. But Tomkins wasn't around to hear. The E. T. agent had turned abruptly and was weaving his way through the crowd, shouting something about being right back.

Hill frowned and turned back to the field. The stadium was emptying quickly. The Rec director stood there for a second, still looking puzzled. Then suddenly he vaulted the low fence around the field, and set off across the grass.

He walked briskly across the stadium and down into the

visitors' locker room. The Brish'diri were changing clothes in sullen silence, and filing out of the room slowly to the airbus that would carry them back to the trade mission.

Remjhard-nei was sitting in a corner of the room.

The Brish'dir greeted him with a slight nod. "Director Hill. Did you enjoy the game? It was a pity our half-men failed in their final test. But they still performed creditably, do you not think?"

Hill ignored the question. "Don't give me the bit about failing, Remjhard. I'm not as stupid as I look. Maybe no one else in the stadium realized what was going on out there this afternoon, but I did. You didn't lose that game. You threw it. Deliberately. And I want to know why!"

Remjhard stared at Hill for a long minute. Then, very slowly, he rose from the bench on which he was seated. His face was blank and expressionless, but his eyes glittered in the dim light.

Hill suddenly realized that they were alone in the locker room. Then he remembered the awesome Brish'diri strength, and took a hasty step backwards away from the alien.

"You realize," Remjhard said gravely, "that it is a grave insult to accuse a Brish'dir of dishonorable conduct?"

The emissary took another careful look around the locker room to make sure the two of them were alone. Then he took another step towards Hill.

And broke into a wide smile when the director, edging backwards, almost tripped over a locker.

"But, of course, there is no question of dishonor here," the alien continued. "Honor is too big for a half-man's play. And, to be sure, in the rules that you furnished us, there was no provisions requiring participants to—" He paused. "—to play at their best, shall we say?"

Hill, untangling himself from the locker, sputtered. "But there are unwritten rules, traditions. This sort of thing simply is not sporting."

Remjhard was still smiling. "To a Brish'dir, there is nothing as meaningless as an unwritten rule. It is a contradiction in terms, as you say."

"But *why*?" said Hill. "That's what I can't understand.

Everyone keeps telling me that your culture is virile, competitive, proud. Why should you throw the game? Why should you make yourself look bad? *Why?*"

Remjhard made an odd gurgling noise. Had he been a human, Hill would have thought he was choking. Instead, he assumed he was laughing.

"Humans amuse me," the Brish'dir said at last. "You attach a few catch phrases to a culture, and you think you understand it. And, if something disagrees with your picture, you are shocked.

"I am sorry, Director Hill. Cultures are not that simple. They are very complex mechanisms. A word like 'pride' does not describe everything about the Brish'diri.

"Oh, we are proud. Yes. And competitive. Yes. But we are also intelligent. And our values are flexible enough to adjust to the situation at hand."

Remjhard paused again, and looked Hill over carefully. Then he decided to continue. "This football of yours is a fine game, Director Hill. I told you that once before. I mean it. It is very enjoyable, a good exercise of mind and body.

"But it is only a game. Competing in games is important, of course. But there are larger competitions. More important ones. And I am intelligent enough to know which one gets our first priority.

"I received word from Brishun this afternoon about the use to which the Kosg-Anjehn victories were being put. Your friend from Extraterrestrial Relations must have told you that I rank among the leaders of the Brish'diri Peace Party. I would not be here on Earth otherwise. None of our opponents is willing to work with humans, whom they consider animals.

"Naturally I came at once to the stadium and informed our half-men that they must lose. And they, of course, complied. They too realize that some competitions are more important than others.

"For in losing, we have won. Our opponents on Brishun will not survive this humiliation. In the next Great Choosing many will turn against them. And I, and others at the mission, will profit. And the Brish'diri will profit.

"Yes, Director Hill," Remjhard concluded, still smiling. "We are a competitive race. But competition for control of a world takes precedence over a football game."

Hill was smiling himself by now. Then he began to laugh. "Of course," he said. "And when I think of the ways we pounded our heads out to think of strategies to beat you. When all we had to do was tell you what was going on." He laughed again.

Remjhard was about to add something when suddenly the locker-room door swung open and Tomkins stalked in. The E.T. agent was still beaming.

"Thought I'd find you here, Hill," he began. "Still trying to investigate those conspiracy theories of yours, eh?" He chuckled and winked at Remjhard.

"Not really," Hill replied. "It was a harebrained theory. Obviously it was the fumble that did it."

"Of course," Tomkins said. "Glad to hear it. Anyway, I've got good news for you."

"Oh? What's that? That the world is saved? Fine. But I'm still out of a job come tonight."

"Not at all," Tomkins replied. "That's what my call was about. We've got a job for you. We want you to join E. T. Relations."

Hill looked dubious. "Come, now," he said. "Me an E. T. agent? I don't know the first thing about it. I'm a small-time local bureaucrat and sports official. How am I supposed to fit into E. T. Relations?"

"As a sports director," Tomkins replied. "Ever since this Brish'diri thing broke, we've been getting dozens of requests from other alien trade missions and diplomatic stations on Earth. They all want a crack at it too. So, to promote goodwill and all that, we're going to set up a program. And we want you to run it. At double your present salary, of course."

Hill thought about the difficulties of running a sports program for two dozen wildly different types of extraterrestrials.

Then he thought about the money he'd get for doing it.

Then he thought about the Starport City Council.

"Sounds like a fine idea," he said. "But tell me. That gravity grid you were going to give to Starport—is that transferable too?''

"Of course," Tomkins said.

'Then I accept." He glanced over at Remjhard. "Although I may live to regret it when I see what the Brish'diri can do on a basketball court."